BORN TO BE WEIRD

A COLLECTION OF DEMENTED

FANTASY & HORROR

SET SYTES

MICROCOSM PUBLISHING
PORTLAND, OR

BORN TO BE WEIRD
A COLLECTION OF DEMENTED FANTASY & HORROR

© Set Sytes, 2016, 2018
This edition © Microcosm Publishing, 2018
First edition, first published 2016
Second Edition, December 2018

ISBN 978-1-62106-475-6
This is Microcosm #287

For a catalog, write or visit:
Microcosm Publishing
2752 N Williams Ave.
Portland, OR 97227
(503)799-2698
MicrocosmPublishing.com

MICROCOSM·PUBLISHING

Microcosm Publishing is Portland's most diversified publishing house and distributor with a focus on the colorful, authentic, and empowering. Our books and zines have put your power in your hands since 1996, equipping readers to make positive changes in their lives and in the world around them. Microcosm emphasizes skill-building, showing hidden histories, and fostering creativity through challenging conventional publishing wisdom with books and bookettes about DIY skills, food, bicycling, gender, self-care, and social justice. What was once a distro and record label was started by Joe Biel in his bedroom and has become among the oldest independent publishing houses in Portland, OR. We are a politically moderate, centrist publisher in a world that has inched to the right for the past 80 years.

THE SCHOOL OF NECROMANCY

I'm here to explain some things to you. A lot of questions have been asked, and a lot of people seem to be pretty concerned, so I have taken it upon myself, when no-one else will, to describe to you the events that led to the six dead bodies found about York last week, which has got the constabulary so vexed. There were, in fact, eight bodies. One was homeless, and the homeless are often forgotten. The other was one of us, and we hold onto our own.

The rules have never said 'Don't talk about the School'. They in fact say, 'We recommend, in your best interests, not to talk about the School, for nobody will take you seriously, and if they do, you are likely to meet an untimely demise.' And so, given that I am confident in my ability to resist the poorly-concocted assassination attempts of my fellows, and even more confident that nobody who reads this will take me seriously (or, if someone does, that nobody will take *them* seriously), I feel like I have nothing to lose by writing this, and I have my own dry amusement to gain, like a serial killer might feel smug upon announcing his morbid deeds to somebody who takes the whole thing as a joke. Doubtless some of my fellows will disagree with me, but they always were a bit fusty and overly serious.

I should point out now that I was not the killer. Just to get that out of your heads. In fact, I wasn't even there, and the story I have to tell is not my own. But I make it my business to know things that happen here, deep under your feet, and I always enjoy interrogating other students.

My name is Raiden Black, and this is not my story.

As an addendum, before I continue, I want to say that *of course* it's not my real name. We are all given new names when we enter the School. Many years ago pretty much half of all the first years would choose 'Black' as their surname, and there was a great deal of names like 'Night' and 'Death' and it all got a bit tedious. Nowadays the masters choose your name for you, and you get three vetoes before you have to suck it up and accept it. I took receiving the now quite elite surname 'Black' as a vote of confidence in me, and have endeavoured to remain deserving of it ever since.

Anyway.

Find a sewer grate or manhole somewhere in York, somewhere in the centre preferably. You will, of course, have to do this at night, unless you are exceptionally quick and daring, or you have found a perfectly hidden spot. Different cliques of students have their own entrances, and if you find yourself sharing yours with a member of The Brotherhood, you have my sympathies.

Head down into the sewers, and head east. Follow the rats. They always seem to congregate around the School, and we never did quite know why they are drawn here so, but we don't complain, not when there are so many post-mortem opportunities at hand.

Eventually you won't need the rats at all, and you can follow your nose. Take the turns where the air is stalest, closest . . . You feel that certain something in the air? You don't know what it is, but you feel it, just like the rats. Seek out the source, for that is us.

Assuming you have a good sense of direction, and have not become irretrievably lost, nor have you been bitten by a rat carrying one of the new experimental strains of plague we have developed, then you should, eventually, come to a door.

It is of heavy wood, and looks ancient, and no amount of battering force will break it open. Here you must knock a certain number of times, to a certain rhythm. And that is one thing I will not tell you.

You can however, assuming you finished reading this *before* you set out, go to the gloomiest pubs in York and, on suitably dark, grim nights, find a sallow youth all in black drinking by himself, looking terribly preoccupied with something, and perhaps a trifle jittery. He will have bags under his eyes from lack of sleep and excess of obsession.

He will at first want nothing to do with you, and will be sullen and uncooperative, but ply him with drinks. At the opportune moment, ask him about the secret knock, and he may tell you.

He will of course be lying. That's one thing we are very good at.

Let's assume, though, that you now know the secret knock, by fair means or foul, and have rapped sharply on the door in this very particular rhythm. The door opens, slowly, with the groan of a thousand years. There is nobody behind it. You may think it black magic, and I wouldn't dare ruin it for you.

You're not at the School yet. Down a spiral staircase of stone steps you go, and as it levels out you find yourself in a series of twisting, crossing corridors. These are the Catacombs of York. Our catacombs.

Set into the walls, lit by burning torches, are all manner of artefacts. You may be surprised to see Egyptian sarcophagi and urns, so far away from their origins, along with Greek burial shrouds, and the beaks of plague doctors from the time of the Black Death.

You will see small cairns, caskets, tools of morticians and torturers, stones and pieces of hard wood with strange carvings, pagan statues, death masks, old coins to lay on eyes, cotton to wrap and minerals to sprinkle on the departed. What you will not see, however, no matter what you will most fearfully open, are bodies, not even skeletons. We have claimed them all, for we do not allow waste.

Navigate the Catacombs (a clue: follow the eyes), and you will find another staircase, which will lead to one final door, requiring a key to unlock. You don't have such a key, you say? That is a shame.

Beyond this door lies the School of Necromancy.

There is also a perfectly serviceable lift that cuts out all this, but let's keep things traditional.

The S.O.N. functions as a school and university both. It teaches students aged, with exceptions of mature students and gifted young prodigies, fifteen to twenty-one or twenty-two; a degree, to those staying on past the age of eighteen, being either a three year or four year course.

The subjects we teach are many, but you will, perhaps, sense a common theme. The first couple of years are chiefly theoretical, apart from groundswork, which is, when you rub away the bullshit, gravedigging. Like most schools and universities, nobody takes first years seriously, no matter how lofty their ambitions. You do the work, and you do it well, without complaining, and you just might rise in estimation.

Apart from groundswork, you will study necrochemistry and necrobiology (nec-chem and nec-bio for short), anatomy, mortuary science, embalming, dissection, cremation, history, gothic art, forensic pathology, elementary reanimation, elementary occultism, and so on. Fairly basic stuff, looking back, and some of us, myself included, felt pretty held back. But of course a lot of us had our wild ideas, and without a solid framework to base them on we may have failed later on.

For every year, including the degree years, you will study and take notes from the many-volumed *Necronomicon*. Not Abdul Alhazred's book, of course, but the *Necronomicon textbook, 7th edition*. In its weighty pages contains just about everything, up to a professional level, to do with treating, understanding, raising, and controlling the dead.

If you choose to do a degree (and some of the less gifted or less ambitious students don't, instead becoming our laboratory assistants or gravediggers), you have a range of subjects to undertake, including: History of the Dead (fusty), History of Necromancy (almost as fusty), Toxicology (poisons), Theoretical Homicide (not *strictly* theoretical), Demonology (a farce), Black Tarot (don't get me started), Mortuary Surgery, Reanimation, Experimental Necroscience, Vampiric Studies, the ever-popular Necromancy, and Necromonology (my chosen degree, which involves the study of and establishing control over the dead, the latter being, in my opinion, an ingredient much missing from my peers' experiments).

The School itself is like an underground castle, or rather network of dungeons, seeing as it is without a top. All work is engaged in underground, with many layers of soil and stone pressing down upon us. Many first years, and some second years, experience what we refer to as 'the underlows', as in 'he can't come to class, he's got a bad case of the underlows'. Eventually almost everyone gets used to it, and you get enough night-time fieldwork (mainly in cemeteries) to give you some fresh air. I never had much problem myself—some of the halls are so huge that you may as well be outside, and I never did miss the sunlight.

Allowing for our various racial skin colour differences, we are by and large a pasty bunch, as you might expect. We get what we need from various tonics and pills, but as the food we acquire (don't ask—you'd be surprised how many associates and graduates of our school are among you) is so excellent, and our scholarly and personal pursuits are so involving (some would say obsessive, and they'd be right), we don't want for much, beyond what we need for our work.

Roam the stone corridors and halls, the tunnels and staircases, the laboratories and cellars and libraries, the crypts, morgues, test chambers, operating theatres and black chapels, and you will cross many paths with the School's prowling cats. There are three of them, or three named ones at least, each as dark as the night. The fat, sluggish one with the unfortunate limp, squashed face and mismatched eyes is affectionately named Igor (and I will happily poison any student who picks on him). Then there are the siblings, Minas and Morgul. Minas is the female, quick and sleek; she sees all, hears all, and every intrepid risk-taking student (the majority of them) who wants to last the course should learn who she's loyal to.

Morgul is the male, and he is really quite huge, more like a panther than a cat, and if you try to kick him you are likely to end up on a dissecting table within the hour.

The students themselves are a mixed bunch. Most of them have black hair, but not as many as used to. In my day it was various shades of black, grey, silver or white, or perhaps, in the case of eccentrics, a very dark brown. These days you'll often see a student with purple, red, green, blue hair and so on, or only streaks of these colours. Some are undyed, and come as blondes and brunettes. I'm not wholly prejudiced, so don't treat them too differently, but I will say if you rock up to a forensic pathology class with bright pink hair, don't be surprised if old Master Scrimpot directs *all* his most difficult questions to you.

We wear a lot of black, true, but there are also a lot of white lab coats worn out of class (some bloodstained), and brown tweed isn't out of the question among some of the more mature students and masters. There are coats and cloaks, robes, three piece suits, shirts and jackets, skirts and dresses, corsets and bodices, lace and leather, soft velvet and jangling chains, and even some bare chests here and there, particularly among groundworkers. Styles are all over the place, though usually on the more gothic, formal, or macabre (if you're trying to be edgy) end of the spectrum. Victorian and Edwardian fashions clash with new pagan which clash with shinobi which clash with new romantic which clash with seventies librarian which clash with thirties suits. And some of us just look like your average Joe/plain Jane. Those are often the ones to watch.

We are generally old-fashioned and semi-traditional, so some of the more radical newer styles are frowned on, and while the dress code is very relaxed, it *is* there. Cybergoggles will be taken off you in class. All in all though, we all look the same in a lab coat and gloves, up to our elbows in body parts.

The Grandmaster is the head of the School of Necromancy, and until you are taking a degree you will probably never see him up close and personal, and even then perhaps not, unless you are of exceptional merit or simply lucky. You can, however, observe him from afar addressing assemblies in the Great Hall, chairing dinners and welcoming each new year. On one wall here is a huge portrait of him: mysterious, cold and elegant, and his personage reflects that. Only absolute fools do not regard him with the utmost respect.

Meet him and you will be forgiven for thinking him a vampire. Rumours get around, too, and first years are often led to believe that he is one. Some impressionable students take to drinking blood and even sharpening their teeth in order to draw his attention. I've tasted one of his red drinks. Cranberry juice. I poisoned it anyway, and he drank it: no effects. I saw him looking at me with a small smile on his face . . . I'd never thought much of my chances, but I think I'd have let him down if I hadn't at least tried. No doubt he's survived hundreds of assassination attempts without even a scar.

Vampire? Not quite, but the truth isn't far off. He definitely has vampiric blood, I think perhaps on his mother's side. You see, these days it's never a matter of 'is he a vampire or isn't he', more a matter of percentage. I have spoken at length with the Master of Vampire Studies, Edwin Cowl, and he is definite that no pure bloods exist anymore in Britain. There were a couple of them, perhaps, a decade ago, visiting London from their home somewhere in Northern Europe, but they were swallowed up and snuffed out like that city does to so many strange folk.

The modern world does not suit their ancient ways. They are an endangered species. I would not be surprised to learn that there were no true vampires in Europe anymore, merely their diluted descendants. Master Cowl told me that there are a few inbreeding vampire families in the backwoods of southern USA, keeping hidden, a few in Russia, and some in the least developed parts of Africa. Apparently China has a vampire family who are actually quite important and powerful. I wonder how long they will last in the spotlight, before their ways are discovered and understood for what they are.

I am digressing, I apologise. You will, perhaps, fully understand when I say that by writing this I am procrastinating on my latest research paper. But all this should give you a flavour of the environment we surround ourselves in, that is so utterly foreign and mythical to you. We are not wizards and witches—at least, we do not think of ourselves as such, despite the occultism—but are scientists, eagerly involving ourselves with the things of the grave, and beyond the grave.

An outsider would think many of us mad, if not all, but you must understand once you have spent time within these walls, so deep below the surface, you too will become infected by the mania that surrounds you, the frenetic drive that propels us to complete our work, pushing us to do more and more, ever greater scientific feats against nature.

We tell time, if needed, by our many clocks, and by the colour of the lights, that shift from white to yellow, to green, then the blue of dawn, then back to white. Not a cycle goes by where you will not hear somewhere an exultant shouting, a frenzied screaming, desperate rages, pleading, or a cry of 'It's ALIVE!—Oh, wait . . . fuck.'

Just remember, whatever you hear and whatever you see, that we're all insomniacs, we're all exhausted, and, disregarding some of our creations, we all are at least mostly human.

There are three main players to my tale, and each of them are third year students. Third years are usually the ones you have the most trouble with. First years are too awed by everything, too meek, and certainly too ignorant of anything remotely necromantic or necro-scientific. Second years are, by and large, eager for knowledge, grasping at anything that give them a foot up, and getting the most out of the classes that are more interesting than those available to first years. It's third year, when most of the students are seventeen, that they get cocky, and think they know enough to tackle their ambitious and naïve ideas.

There is Henry Graves. A quiet, pleasant lad, with a mess of dusky hair that falls about his face. He studies with moderate effort, gets average grades, and is tolerable enough that he hasn't had a single attempt made on his health by another student. He would not, I'm sure he won't mind me saying, be particularly notable if not for his acquaintance with Arthur Pale, and his subsequent involvement in the events to come.

Arthur is, or should I say was, slightly obnoxious. He was small and reedy-voiced, with a pinched face and short mousy hair, and he was also a know-it-all, who, as is often the case, didn't actually know as much as he thought he did. Events have certainly demonstrated he lacked wisdom. He was ambitious to a fault, one of those in the School who forewent both sleep and their assignments in order to pursue their own private research. The lack of rest never seemed to exhaust him, although he was a jittery, quick-talking sort, and he put most other students slightly on edge being around him for any length of time. He'd put his hand up in class over and over, or plain interrupt the master, to the point that even a couple of the masters had tried to poison or entrap him, to teach him a lesson if nothing else.

Nevertheless, he had emerged from every attempt by student or master unscathed and unbothered, and he would not deign to even remark on them, annoying people further. He sat by himself in classes until a particular day, mid-year, that he was found lab-partnered with another, and without comment the two stayed at each other's side every single day.

This man, for it is a grown man, was called Shade. A strong name, if I do say so, although nobody knew his first name, not even the masters, and I expect not even himself. Neither did anyone, except possibly the Grandmaster, know his age, for while he was clearly an older student, he had that kind of face that almost defies age, and he could well be anywhere from twenty to forty.

Shade was an enigma, principally so because he almost never spoke, except possibly in private. He would certainly not speak up in front of a group, and if asked a question in class, as I once did (taking the class when the master was indisposed), he would stare right at you and say nothing until you moved to somebody else. Not that mutes were rare in the School, but there was something singular about Shade. He was very tall, and always wore a dark brown buttoned-up jacket with a wide-knot tie, a bowler hat that hid a bald head, and wire silver spectacles that were tinted a deep, cloudy purple. On the occasions he removed his glasses, such as to put on required goggles, his eyes were large and a piercing light blue.

There was something slightly wolfish about his face, giving rise to ridiculous rumours about him being a werewolf (students in this place can get carried away with it all). But, oddly enough, he was actually rather handsome. I say oddly, because Shade became a permanent laboratory assistant and dogsbody to Arthur Pale, never seeming to want anything more, and while it may be rather stereotypical of me to say, most dyed-in-the-wool lab assistants are ugly, often deformed in some way. Whether they are or not, they are always the less gifted of students, and Mr Shade's bright blue eyes always did betray to me a calm, yet sharp intelligence that was never spoken.

You may wonder that I have not told you anything about our selection process, how students ever come here when our organisation and practices are so secretive, and when we are not being secretive we are being misunderstood. This is one thing I will not divulge; merely I will tell you that our students are chosen, and those that reject our offer do not end up speaking of it to others.

And now you have some idea to the background, and the principal players at hand, I will not delay you further, and I will begin this story, as has come to my knowledge piece by piece. I hope my penchant for storytelling does not get in the way of the facts.

It was two months ago that the accident befell Arthur Pale, and Henry Graves was there to witness it. It had been one chilly night, the halogens glowing green from the ceilings and walls, that Henry walked along the corridor towards the Great Hall, where the sounds of merriment were underway.

Not all students took themselves seriously all the time, and those that were not hard at work were feasting and drinking. Tonight was some celebration, the anniversary of the biggest mass resurrection in the School's history. Not that the students carousing cared about that; they only needed the excuse.

The first drifts of a song reached Henry's ears, and he smiled. It was a drinking song that everybody knew off by heart, whether they wanted to or not.

Oh, the grand old Duke of York,

He had ten thousand men;

He shot them down—then he raised them up!

Then he shot them down again.

And when they were dead they were dead,

And when they were not they were not,

And when they were only half-way dead—

'They were neither dead nor not,' Henry finished, to himself. There were many other verses and variants, that students over the years had concocted, but this was the only one that everybody could join in on. Few knew any more than what the song said about the whole debacle. Henry did though. Henry had read the restricted books. He knew the *original*.

He looked in as he approached the Hall, seeing mugs quaffed and stamped on the wooden tables, and the throng launched themselves into a repeat of the song, this time louder and with more emphasis on choice bits. Henry hovered there for a second, contemplating joining, but he felt like a late arrival to pierce the knot of students, and far too sober to begin. Most of them were second years too, he noticed, and he shrugged his shoulders and continued on.

His walk was aimless, and while he made an impromptu decision that he would head to the nearest library (for there were four in the College, dealing with different branches of our work), he found himself walking past the entrance without so much as a hesitation. He strode on, into parts of the School seldom walked, down a twisting staircase, past the black and white cinema that flickered through pictures from the 20s and 30s, and past the crematorium (rarely used, as I have mentioned before that we do not waste, and when a corpse or body part has exhausted its potential there are always abominations in the cellars that need feeding, some of whom have the capability to devour bone).

It was then that he heard the talk, the quick and excited yet demanding chatter of one of his peers, and upon further steps forward he recognised the voice as belonging to Arthur Pale.

Henry Graves understood now that he was approaching one of the old test chambers, used only for historical demonstrations, due to the antiquity of the equipment. This was where the words were coming from, and as Henry tip-toed closer it went as follows:

'Plug the seventh wire in Shade, the seventh! Now turn the dial to one-hundred-and-eighty-six-point-three. Point three, not a fraction less! That's it! That's it! Can you see Shade, it's glowing!'

'Yes Master,' a second voice joined the first, low and guttural.

'Those fools abandoning this place, don't they know what this machine can *do*? Simpletons! There's power here that would dwarf their absurd reanimations and chemical ineffectualities! Turn the dial point four more Shade!'

'Yes Master.'

'The Mark Six solution, the pangrenic, it's bubbling hard, the beauty! Let me just add the catalyst . . . In a second it'll turn bright orange, just you wait!'

'Master . . .'

'Not now Shade, you fool! This needs every last fibre of my being attentive to this task! Here we go . . . steady does it . . .'

Henry Grave put his head around the doorway and for a brief second saw Arthur Pale standing on a footstool, a test tube in his trembling hand, tipping it towards a complicated apparatus of silver spirals and winding tubes, his goggles half-steamed from the bubbling beaker he leant towards, and Shade, standing a few feet back, his face turned away, his expression impenetrable behind those purpled spectacles; all this in a second, before the explosion shattered glass and scalding green liquid in all directions.

Henry lowered his shielding arm, and rushed in. Arthur and Shade were on the ground. Arthur was twitching, face down.

Shade got to his feet at Henry's approach and, ignoring him, moved to Arthur. If he was hurt then he didn't show it.

'Arthur?' Henry said, tentatively, and then, as Shade grabbed Arthur's arm and turned him roughly over, Arthur screamed in their faces, a howling, half-gurgling and torturous sound that rent Henry's ears and still keeps him awake to this day; the mad sounds of unbridled agony ever echoing.

Arthur's eyes were wide in horror, staring at Henry's face, or rather only one eye did, for the other was the colour of rancid milk, completely blinded; half his face melting down onto his shirt collar like hot, buttery wax, and nobody and nothing to save him.

Henry found himself slammed against a pillar. Shade, his glasses fallen off and his eyes boring like veins of ice into Henry's brain, had grabbed him by the neck.

'*LEAVE,*' bellowed Shade in a voice from a tomb.

Henry ran.

It was a fortnight later that anybody saw Arthur Pale. His appearance had scarcely improved. The right side of his face was permanently disfigured; his right eye would never see anything again. The melt of his face had hardened in drips and globules, and a master had been forced to saw through it where it had stuck fast to his collar. His lips had not burned away but drooped down on the side, nearly to the bottom of his chin, like an unfinished effigy of a clown in a grotesque parody of sadness. Depending on the light his visage looked like wet leather or glue, like it would come away on your hands if you touched it, like if you watched him for long enough you could see his whole gelatinous profile drop all the way to the floor.

Needless to say if they sat away from him before, now students went out of their way to avoid him. There were few in the School who did not regard him with disgust and horror, however much they might attempt to conceal it. Disfigurements were common in the School, and there were plenty of students with burns and scars and mottled skin, hair lips and false eyes, humps and limps, missing fingers or disjointed arms, but Arthur Pale was something else entirely, and crossing him on claustrophobic spiral staircases, in the shadows of the morgues or between the stacks of the libraries was enough to give not only the first years nightmares.

Arthur roamed the School more than ever, but he was absent from all classes. Nobody complained, and even the masters breathed a sigh of relief. Only one person stuck by his side, and that was the indomitable Shade.

Before Arthur's accident, there had been only one person apart from Shade that he had thought fondly of, and that person was Mistress Veil—Anola Veil. Do not let all my talk of masters make you think the S.O.N. is a wholly patriarchal organisation. It certainly began that way, and traditions run long and stiff down here, but every mistress is considered one of the masters, and it is correct to refer to them as both mistress and master, although when addressing one most still use the former, out of habit if nothing else. There are six female masters in the School, but it is only Mistress Veil we are interested in right now. Or rather, that Arthur was interested in.

Unfortunately his feelings were never reciprocated. Even if there wasn't a rule against master-student relations (the existence of which was quite forgotten about, as the inhabitants of the School are usually far too busy with other things to pursue sexual ambitions), who could fancy poor, irritating, reedy-voiced, ratty-faced Arthur Pale? Certainly not the cold beauty of Anola Veil, with her black gowns, her bluish-white hair like a frozen waterfall, her heavy-lidded eyes that blinked slow and indolently at you as you talked. She was the Master of Necromonology (a position I am grooming myself for), and she also taught gothic art and elementary and advanced occultism, besides being generally adept in all other disciplines. When she had substituted for the sick leave (an ogre of a creation had ripped his arm off) of the master of Theoretical Homicide . . . well, I'll never forget her classes, let's just say.

I fancied her myself, you know, but none of us got close to her (or if somebody did then she removed the evidence *completely*). Then again, I used to fancy almost everyone, and if you'd have asked me back then I'd have said the same as I tell you now—Anola Veil couldn't hold a candle to the Mistress of Black Tarot, Angelina Heartspike, who was and still is a simply bewitching wildcat, no matter how little I think of her chosen mastery. But Anola was terribly intelligent and exceptionally independent, and quite unattainable even to the best of us, so, you will understand when I say Arthur Pale, even before the incident, didn't have a chance in Hell, and observing his sycophantic attempts to ingratiate himself with her were quite embarrassing.

Mistress Veil was the only person bar Shade who Arthur continued to speak to after the accident. She, to her credit, never recoiled from him, but neither was she anything approaching warm. The less she gave him the more he would press her; into answering questions that may or may not have been related to his research, into answering questions about herself (little forthcoming), into coming to help him study (refused), and even into going to eat with him in his room. Eventually Anola's patience ran thin, and she told him in no uncertain terms to drop the entire charade and not to bother her with this nonsense again. At this Arthur's dropped his tortured countenance, and without another word strode off, Shade not a few steps behind.

Two days later, when Anola was to deliver her gothic art class to a group of third years, she was absent.

Henry Graves had been in that class, and, while other students trickle by trickle drifted out, disappointed (nobody missed Anola's classes), he stayed sitting, his expression worried. He had this awful feeling, a feeling that soon people were going to start looking, looking and not finding. A feeling that there might be one person who would know where she was, and that this person wasn't going to tell the truth. His feelings were based on gut, and not evidence, but the gut is a powerful thing, involving a wisdom deeper than our conscious mind can comprehend, and it was powerful enough to take Henry out of that chair and that classroom and up staircases and along corridors and past a black chapel, its gargoyles ever watching, past the open door of Laboratory 18, where Master Sepul was instructing first years how to make the lump of beaten flesh jerk just *so*, past the entrance to the third year dormitories, down a long, sloping tunnel, and on to the dripping depths of the eastern wing where the outcast Arthur Pale now lived.

Henry knocked on the door timidly. Nothing happened and he knocked louder, and the door jerked open two inches. *The good side*, thought Henry, as he looked into Arthur Pale's mistrustful eye and tense half-mouth.

'*You*,' said Arthur.

'Yes,' said Henry.

The door opened wider, and Henry swallowed as he faced the part of Arthur that was a monster. Behind Arthur the room was swallowed in gloom, but for the bloom of a yellow light in the corner. Shade stood by the light; silent, looming and still.

'What do you want?'

'Do you . . . do you have any idea where Mistress Veil might be? She didn't turn up to class. She always turns up.'

Arthur's surviving eyebrow narrowed. 'What makes you think I'd know?'

'I don't. I'm just asking. I know how fond you are of her.'

'What makes you think that?'

'Everyone knows.' Now Henry's eyes had adjusted a little, there seemed to be something, some shape in the bed. 'Is someone else here? Apart from Shade.'

Arthur's eye twitched. 'No. Now go away, I have work to do.' He made to close the door, but Henry, in a sudden spasm of suspicion, shoved the door open, and it banged against the wall.

Arthur made a noise of anger but Henry had already brushed past him, seeing the figure lying under the blanket, her snowfall hair unmistakeable.

He clapped a hand to his mouth. 'What have you done?' he whispered.

Arthur grabbed his arm tightly. 'You wouldn't understand.'

Henry's eyes met Arthur's. He looked mad, feverish. 'You were . . . sleeping with her body?' Henry managed.

Arthur's fingers clenched harder, his nails digging in. 'She *denied* me!' he hissed. 'She was never going to accept me. I *wasted* so much time on her. But it won't be for nothing. I have her now. She can be mine whenever I want.'

'Arthur, don't you think people will realise? You can't keep her here without . . . without someone finding out . . . she's a master, they don't just go missing without comment!'

'Of *course* they do, you idiot! Four years ago the Master of Necrochemistry simply vanished, never to be heard from again. Seven years ago the Master of Vampiric Studies, on field research in northern Russia, never came back. Twelve years ago the Master of Ghoul Studies, all they found of her was her bloodstained shoes. These things *happen.* In a place like this you almost expect them to happen. I think it's high time another one went, don't you? Who better than the *favourite* Anola Veil?'

'She'll *rot* Arthur! She'll decompose! What, are you stealing supplies to keep her fresh? How long can you keep this up?'

'Haven't you learned *anything* in this School Henry? I'll bring the bitch to life! I'll bring her back and she will know *me* as her master! She will do anything I say . . .'

'That's beyond our skills, we're only third years! Bringing back a whole body, permanently, a master at that . . . you don't know what you're doing!'

Arthur's good eye rolled and the left side of his mouth curled. 'It may be beyond you, but it's not beyond *me*.' He lightly stroked his waxwork face, and shuddered. 'I won't be disfigured for nothing Henry. I'm working on my Mark Seven . . . this time it'll work. It'll work, and combined with the right incantations Mistress Veil will very soon be more lively than she ever was in life.'

Henry shook his arm free of Arthur's grip. He opened his mouth to say something when Arthur cut in.

'I know what you're thinking Henry. You're thinking about telling on me. Of course. Except, you won't, will you?' He beckoned behind him, and Shade moved closer, towering over them both. His eyes stared into Henry's own, forceful and strong and yet almost unseeing.

'Shade is a good assistant,' Arthur continued. 'He's awfully loyal. He holds my books and my potions. He fetches and carries. You wouldn't believe how strong he is. He takes care of things that need taken care of. I'd hate to have to ask him to take care of something so . . . insalubrious. There's already one body . . .' He gestured to the woman in the bed. 'I wouldn't want to add another.'

Henry said nothing, and Arthur put a hand on his shoulder, ushering him out the door. 'I think it's time you got back to your own work, don't you Henry? I'm sure there's lots to be done. You get back to your work . . . and I'll get back to mine.'

Henry couldn't sleep that night. The following day, as soon as the lamps turned from blue to white, he ignored his classes and went back to find Arthur. He banged and banged on the door but nobody answered. He put his ear to the wood and listened, but there was only an eerie silence. He visited the old test chamber, that horrible scene of which he was reminded of every time he looked at Arthur Pale's face. It was empty. Eventually he returned to his room and ruminated.

He tried to concentrate on his studies, but it was no use. By the time the lights shifted yellow to green, and in the outside world all was dark, Henry had left his room again and gone back to Arthur's for another attempt. He raised his fist to knock at the same time as the door swung open, and Arthur and Shade walked out.

Arthur didn't look surprised to see him, and Shade had never looked surprised. Arthur clapped a hand on his neck. 'You're just in time my friend!' he announced. Shade took Henry very firmly by the arm and between them they marched Henry along the corridor.

'In time for what? Where are you going?' said Henry nervously. He tried to shake free from Shade but it was no use, the grip was iron.

'Where are *we* going,' corrected Arthur. 'We're going to the surface.'

'The surface? Why?'

'Why, dear Henry, that's where Mistress Veil is.'

'How in the hell did she get up there?'

'Shade buried her in the cemetery last night. After we pumped her . . . with Mark Seven, that is.' Arthur smiled, or at least half of him did, and it looked truly horrible. It was then that Henry noticed that he was carrying a book under one arm. A large, black book, its cover littered with silver hieroglyphics.

'You're going to raise her up there?'

Arthur patted the book. 'It's the way it has to be done. In a cemetery. Dead of night. We're doing it the real way, the old way.'

'You don't know what you're doing. Please see sense Arthur. You've no idea what might happen. You can turn back now, and we'll forget the whole thing, I'll say I have no idea where she went . . .'

'Shush now,' said Arthur, and Shade growled.

They didn't come up the sloping tunnel that led away from the east wing, but headed up a thin, straight staircase with high crooked steps. White moss lined the walls and they brushed through cobwebs. It seemed to go on forever, climbing up and up, and pretty soon Henry's legs were aching. Arthur was also breathing hard, taking off his coat, but Shade wasn't even breaking a sweat and his jacket remained buttoned-up to the top.

Finally, the steps shallowed out into a small dusty tunnel, and Arthur and Henry collapsed, while Shade stood over them, staring down the tunnel to the door at the end.

'I don't . . . don't know how he does it,' wheezed Arthur. 'And to think he did this last night . . . carrying a body. It didn't leak, did it Shade?'

'No Master.'

After a couple more minutes Arthur got to his feet, and Shade dragged Henry up. Shade went to the door and pushed it slowly open; it squealed in protest.

Henry looked about him, at the primeval art painted on the walls, at the artefacts set into the walls, suddenly recognising the surroundings. 'This is part of the Catacombs,' he said.

Nobody answered.

Shade led them through the twists and turns, the forks and the crossroads, and their path got narrower and narrower, the ceiling lower with every step. They started to hunch, starting with Shade and ending with Arthur, until they were all bent double. Then Shade took to his knees, and within minutes they were all crawling along. On either side were the smallest urns and grey phials, rolls of wispy string, sitting pygmy skeletons moulded from some strange pale clay that grinned as the trio shuffled by. Strange statues of things with too many limbs, of hollowed out breasts and groins; statues with no heads, or made of only heads.

Shade straightened up in front of them and immediately began to climb. Henry was next, standing up and arching his back and then, as Arthur dogged his heels, climbing the long ladder up to the surface.

He'd never been so pleased to feel the fresh night air. Arthur, too, sucked it in greedily, while looking about him, his eye alive with excitement.

They were in the cemetery. Shade closed the hatch down after them, and it became just another grave tablet. *In Honoured Memory of* . . . well, I won't be telling you the name. Let's not make things too easy for anybody who wants to do a little exploring.

They wandered the graves, following Shade. Henry contemplated making a run for it—Shade may be strong, but was he fast? But his legs kept moving in Shade's wake, Arthur just behind him. There was part of him that wanted to be here, that wanted to see what would happen. He was in third year and yet had still never seen a whole body raised perfectly back to life, only teases of it. And that book Arthur carried . . . he just knew it was filled with occult magic, with black secrets even those older students taking advanced degrees in Demonology and Necromancy weren't allowed to read. It whispered to him of death and life, of the voids of space and time, of other worlds, of creatures living in the gaps of the world, waiting to come out. He was afraid and excited at once.

'Where did you get that book?' he said, as they stopped at an unmarked grave, lit only by the orb of a full moon.

Arthur didn't reply, but Henry didn't really need him to. He knew it was Anola Veil's, stolen from her private quarters. Perhaps she was reading it when Shade had knocked on her door, his hands tense and clenching, his face expressionless.

Arthur opened the book, his own hands trembling just as they had trembled holding the test tube, the solution that had exploded when he poured, turning him into somebody's nightmare.

Henry looked at the pages, but found the text indecipherable, the letters alien to him. 'You can read it?'

'Well enough,' replied Arthur. He started to read.

If the letters were alien, hearing the words spoken was doubly so. Henry would never be able to remember those words, but nor would he ever be able to shake off the *feel* of them; those monstrous, clicking and gnashing syllables that seemed to fight their way through Arthur's mouth, the fog of dread that wisped its way up through the ground and into their lungs and hearts, the sudden dank chill of the night, the awful corpulence of the moon as it bulged and breathed.

'STOP!' Henry cried, but it was clear that Arthur couldn't even if he had wanted to. More horrible words, so unnatural to the human vocal cords, tripped and danced out of his gibbering mouth, until it was that the book snapped shut with a bang and fell to the floor, and the incantation was done.

Silence reigned.

Then the earth shifted under their feet. A fingernail, then a hand. Then an arm, not in black silk, but a navy coat, dirt falling off it as it rose; the fingers clawing at the air, the flesh as white as bone.

'Shade . . . who is this . . .' said Arthur, and for once Shade did not answer him.

The body came up through the soil, just to the left of the unmarked grave, and it was not Mistress Anola Veil.

The fingers adjusted the worn medals that hung limply off the military coat, adjusted the dull gold buttons, adjusted the threadbare epaulettes, adjusted the collar where the head should have been.

The fingers tapped the opening. Not a neck, but a pink gibbosity, a writhing tumour with fat red veins pulsating. It reacted to the touch, and protrusions appeared; it began to swell out in different directions, as though inside limbs were trying to push themselves out.

'It's . . . it's . . .' started Arthur Pale.

'I know what it is,' said Henry quietly, the horror climbing over him like a spider. 'It's the Duke of York.'

'The . . . ?'

'*That* Duke of York. You read the *wrong fucking spell*!'

'What? Of the celebration, the song? The biggest mass resurrection . . . The Grand Old Duke of York, he had ten thousand men . . .'

'It's not a celebration you idiot! It's a *warning*! We just forgot, we all forgot! And they're not the original lines!'

And in a slow, sonorous voice, Shade began to chant.

The grand old Duke of York

He had ten thousand dead

He raised them up

Then took them out

With a spell that blew his head.

And when they were gone they were gone

And the same was said for him.

Something had come

From beyond the sun

And crawled into his skin.

The creature's tumescent protrusions were now thick tendrils, a dozen of them, waving and flicking about, reaching higher and higher. By the time Shade had finished his chant the tendrils were several feet above the body, and the swollen base glowed and trembled with an unearthly light.

'There's more than just the dead and living out there!' cried Henry, as he and Arthur began to back away. 'There's *things* . . . Every time the Duke shot one of the men that he had awakened, they just came back! Maybe there was ten thousand, maybe it was just a hundred, or a dozen, but there were too many for him to handle. He turned to a book . . . *your* book!'

'You could have told me!' moaned Arthur, as his back hit a gravestone.

'I didn't know till now! How was I to know Shade picked the same damn spot to bury Veil as the Duke of York!'

'I didn't know either! I didn't know he was buried here!'

'The spell was too powerful. It destroyed all the zombies -'

'We're not supposed to use that word . . .'

'Shut up! It destroyed them all but it was too powerful, it created a rift . . . a portal to . . . nobody knows where, but something came through . . . Arthur it stole his soul! It replaced him, it wore his skin!'

Shade was still standing in front of the Duke, staring at it as its fleshy pink snakes whipped about, lashing the air, and from in its chest there came a moaning and chittering noise that rose in intensity.

'Shade get out of there!' yelled Arthur, as they moved back further, trying to navigate the gravestones without turning their back on the thing. Shade looked behind, and one of the tendrils flicked out and wrapped itself to his throat.

'SHADE!'

The creature yanked him forward, and Shade was thrown to the ground, slithering through dirt to the feet of the thing. His hat and glasses had come off, revealing his shining eyes and perfectly bald dome. He got up, unsteadily, and then he pulled the slimy limb that held him to his mouth, where he bit through it in a spray of yellow pus and ichor.

The thing screamed then, so high pitched and so loud that it was amazing it didn't wake half of York. It never came up in the newspapers, and perhaps any that did hear it put it down to a dream, or the sound was so wretched and impossible to human ears that the brain could not, or would not, store it in memory. It was only Henry, whom I questioned at length (along with what little I could get from the taciturn Mr Shade and the reticent Grandmaster), who made mention of it, and with all the other associations with that terrible night I am not surprised it is forever burned into his mind.

It was then that Shade ran, away from the others, the dismembered constrictor falling to the floor where it curled and twitched. The creature followed, lurching and bobbing at a speed equal to Shade's. It must have had capacity for sight, for it dodged gravestones with ease, and followed Shade to the gate of the cemetery.

Henry ran after, and Arthur joined him at a distance. He saw Shade, with three hard kicks, break open the locked iron gates, and shivered at the force behind those kicks. After that they couldn't keep pace, and Shade and the abomination from beyond were lost to the shadows of the streets.

They moved on cautiously, sticking to the streetlights.

'How did it die?' whispered Arthur.

'The last time? The Duke was already dead. His head was blown off by the spell. The creature came into him, but it did not come fast enough. It cannot give its own life to the body, and it was too weak to make it on its own. It needed the host. The necromancers who found the Duke, and all those hundreds or thousands or however many dead bodies lying about him . . . they saw the thing that had taken residence in him. I saw a drawing in a book. The body lying on the ground, the feelers squirming from the headless neck.'

'And?'

'They cut off the feelers. Burned them, I think. Maybe they thought it was dead then, maybe they didn't. Nothing like this had happened before. And then they buried it. In an unmarked grave. Nobody knew where.'

'Until now.'

'Until now.'

It was two hours, a whole exhausting two hours of walking and running up and down streets, along narrow cobbled paths, past sleeping houses and garden shadows, looking and listening, before they saw any evidence they were on the right track. Henry Grave's skin prickled as he looked at the glistening ichor that lay slowly bubbling on the road, next to a hand that had been twisted off at the wrist, leaking the same yellow blood.

'Good on you Shade,' Arthur murmured.

It was then the scream came; not another otherworldly caterwaul, but a human scream of absolute, unique terror.

The two of them shared a look, and then ran as one towards the sound, which abruptly cut out.

They sprinted down the road, rounded a corner, and saw a dead body on the ground. A young woman, walking home from a night, confronted by a monster who had wrapped its tendrils around her throat. Squeezing and squeezing. The head had rolled a few feet away, popped from her neck. Blood coated the ground.

'The newspapers are going to have a field day with this,' said Arthur.

Henry ran a hand through his hair and tried not to look at the expression on the head. 'The Grandmaster really won't like this. Come on, it can't be far off. We have to stop it before it kills more.'

'And how do you propose we do that?'

'I don't know. But this is your mess and you better damn well be prepared to clean it up whatever the cost.'

Arthur didn't reply, but followed Henry as he tracked the intermittent drops of ichor on the ground. Twice they lost the trail, only to backtrack and find it again, travelling in another direction. Time was falling away from them. They had no idea how far off dawn might be, how far off it might be before the police force were roused, and the people of York made aware of the headless darkness that preyed on their streets.

And the School, Henry thought. *The School must be protected. The people cannot—must not—find the source.*

Another hour passed, following trails of blood and screams and unbelieving shouts; strange chittering and wet, slapping noises that were always further off than they seemed. Two more bodies were found, a man and woman together, one decapitated and the other . . . the other with every limb torn from the socket. Her head was still attached, but from the eyes, nostrils and mouth poured a yellow-white foam that congealed glutinously on the tarmac.

Henry put his face in his hands. 'What were you *thinking*!' he shouted at Arthur, who had reached a new level of paleness. 'Raising the dead . . . and with that book! And for what, for sex? For power? Is that it? These deaths are on your hands! And what's worse, the fate of the whole School!'

Arthur opened his mouth to respond, but clapped it shut again when they heard a roar from the adjacent street.

Henry took off, jumping a fence and running through someone's garden. He ran across the road and into a small play park where the thing that was once the Duke of York stood flailing, handless, leaking its juices and thrashing its tentacles in all directions. At its feet was a fourth victim in pieces, presumably human in its scattered mush and meat, and battling the beast with a huge gatepost in his grip was Shade.

Henry wanted to rush in, to help, but he was frozen solid. What chance did he have against this monstrosity? He saw Shade battering the thing with wicked sweeps that would have felled a horse. The demon was weeping yellow, making perverted squeals and tremulous screeches that sounded like nails on a blackboard. The tentacles were nearly twice as long as before, reaching up high into the night; each birthing others, like the branches of a tree. The bulge in the neck had grown into a pustulous sack, and was glowing brighter than ever, resonating with an unknown frequency. The glow shifted through green, to blue, to purple and to the red of fresh blood.

A newly formed tendril squirmed its way along the grass towards Henry's feet, and he stamped on it fiercely and hurried to just behind Shade.

'You're winning!' he said, in desperate encouragement.

'No,' said Shade, batting away a tentacle. 'Gets stronger.'

'We have to beat it Shade. It's killed four people now.' Henry ducked as Shade moved his arm back for a big swing.

'Seven,' said Shade.

'Are you kidding?!'

Shade didn't answer, but three faceless snakes grabbed the fence post and with a burst of enormous strength tore it from him, and the piece of wood sailed out into the night. They slashed at his face, and they got behind him and tripped him. Before Henry could even cry out Shade was a mass of wriggling pink, and only his eyes were visible, before they closed shut.

'NO!'

Henry span to see Arthur racing towards them. 'Stay back!' he cried, but it was no use. Arthur punched the creature in its side with all his might, and it swatted him away as though he were a fly. Arthur got to his feet and ran in again, and two tendrils, two thin, sharp, sickly pink tendrils shot out from the bulb of the neck, daggered out to his face and punctured his eyes.

Arthur Pale gurgled; that was the only sound he made as the feelers pushed themselves into his brain, and vile foamy liquid began to froth around his nostrils and mouth. A tiny, pathetic gurgle, like a baby.

Arthur fell to the ground.

Henry Graves looked in on sheer terror, and in his mind came a single thought. *It's all over. Run.* He turned fast and shrieked as he went slap bang into something, someone.

Hard hands were placed on his shoulder, and he gazed up into a tight-lipped and lined face, and imperious dark eyes. 'Stay here and do nothing,' the mouth said.

' . . . How?' managed Henry.

The Grandmaster looked down his nose at him. 'Do you really think a master can go missing, and only students notice? You are not the only one who can follow a trail.'

He said this quickly and abruptly, and pushed Henry behind him, stepping forward with hands out, wrists pointing towards the abomination, fingers leaning back and curled like the claws of a beast.

The Grandmaster began to incant. Henry recognised them as the same terrible language from the book; surely not meant for the human tongue, not meant for such a naïve, meddling, greedy and covetous people.

The thing, caught in sucking the lifeblood of Arthur Pale dry, must have known the words too, for it withdrew itself and turned to approach the Grandmaster.

It took a step, and another. That was when the mass of tendrils that was Shade began to spurt blood. A yellow blood . . . the snakes started to flee, but the slaughter was just beginning; this was the feast of Shade. Without sound he wrenched his arms free of the loosening mass, and started to cram them in; his jaw gnawing and gnashing in frenzy. The spurt turned into a fountain, an overflowing cauldron of alien blood.

The thing was screeching and howling, too preoccupied with trying to pull its limbs away from Shade's teeth to fight back. Arthur lay on his back, broken eyes drooling the creature's plasm, facing it all and yet seeing nothing. The left side of his face shrivelled, near mummified; now he was both halves the horror.

The Grandmaster clapped his hands. The incantation complete.

There was no scream, no cry out from that thing beyond the sun. Suddenly the world was cast in silence, all breath suspended, all motion muted. Every tentacle and tendril, thick and thin, freshly formed and thick and leathery, shot straight upwards, every single one pointing up at the moon.

And then, slowly but surely, inch by inch, they sank; retreating into the veined bulb from which they'd came.

Henry and the Grandmaster watched, and Shade got up, a trifle unsteadily, and stood by them too, drenched in yellow ichor. His face was grim and flat as usual, no evidence that he'd come close to death at the hands of a swarm of tentacles, but glancing at him Henry swore there was something alight and dancing in his eyes.

The wait was torturous, never knowing if the creature was finally defeated; it may have been only a minute before there was nothing but a pink mound in the neck, and then nothing at all, but it felt like hours, days, a lifetime in the moonlight shadow of evil.

The body of the Duke of York slumped to the ground, once again lifeless.

'Is it dead?' Henry breathed.

'We can never be sure if the host has completely left the body,' said the Grandmaster calmly. 'We must take it to the crematorium.'

'You're taking it into the School?'

'The thing is either dead or retreated to a near nothing. It will not be coming back for a long time, and in a few hours it will not be coming back at all. Shade, please carry the bodies, and walk with me. Dawn is coming, and we must get underground without any more attention.'

Shade stooped and picked up the headless body, and laid it on top of Arthur Pale. He bent down and lifted both bodies up, grunting slightly, but standing up straight. And so the four moved on—the Grandmaster, Shade, and the dead bodies of the Duke and Arthur Pale—with nobody paying any further attention to Henry Graves.

Henry walked a few steps behind, pretending he was an invisible ear, listening hard and trying to catch the words the Grandmaster murmured.

'All these deaths, Shade . . . this does not look good. Please . . . please be more careful in future with whom you spend your time with. Not everybody is worthy of you.'

'Yes Master,' Shade said in a dull monotone.

The Grandmaster peered into Shade's blue eyes. 'Tell me Mr Shade, are you happy here?'

'Yes Master.'

'The other students do not . . . make fun?'

'No Master.'

'Then you do not regret me enrolling you in the School.'

'No Master.'

'Good. That is good.' The Grandmaster straightened, satisfied. He placed a hand on Shade's hard shoulder and walked him along the road, their footfall silent as the grave.

'This was just a hiccup,' the Grandmaster said softly, reassuringly. 'A temporary issue. I'm still exceptionally proud of you Shade. You'll always be my finest creation.'

'Yes Master.'

My account has come to an end, and it is just as well, for it is getting late. It will not be long before the green halogen at my desk glows its sapphiric blue. I must be heading out. I need to reach the surface—I think, this time, I will take the lift—and deliver my report to the likeliest looking drunk I find. The sort that might entertain a conspiracy, that might rant and rave to all about, that will wave these papers in faces that pull back, aghast. Yes, you reading this, if you have got this far. I wish you the best of luck.

I have scented the paper itself with alcohol—it reeks like a brewery—and the paper itself is quite rare; combustible, you know, and such that it will react to sunlight. When dawn comes this account will soon be nought but ash. I'm afraid if you wish to alert the world, you don't have much time.

A waste, you say? Nonsense. A good joke is never a waste.

Raiden Black

Necromonologist

KEEP IT CLEAN

He'd have liked to say that from first look it was just an ordinary toilet, no more homicidal than any other, but he'd have been lying. It was, in fact, the lord of toilets, or its most low-born, its befouled emperor or its most grotesque assassin. Was it cherished, worshipped and obeyed? Did it head the assembly, chair the meetings? Or was it tolerated—barely—by the others, only as needs must; kept in the dark, in the shadows, ugly and deformed even by its own kind. Perhaps it was both, for in such an underworld the forms of power come naturally feculent, a triumph of disgust to the masses that lurked there in their cubicles and private rooms. The gilded and implacable, perfumed and cushioned at the foot, lid closed in deference as muchs as the fetid sinkholes with their vacant dribbling stares.

Whatever its position among them it was one powerful and feared. Its mouth was wide open in a toothless yawn, beckoning him on. He almost made to turn and leave, to hold it in, but he was desperate. If only the pub's bathroom hadn't been out of order. His friends were the ones who had told him to go to the public toilet in Piss Alley—that's what they called this stretch of lightless cobbles, on account of all the homeless were scared of the toilet too, rather letting their urine run down the street than open that door. They knew better.

He'd had to walk past them, and they'd stretched out their hands to him, trying to tug on his jacket. They weren't the usual fallen on hard times, but elephant men, leprous deformities huddled in rags untouched by moonlight. This was their Piss Alley and in the small hours he knew they prostrated themselves before the toilet; their whimpers reached him even in his dreams.

Call it a dodgy curry, IBS, or a reaction to the alcohol: a cauldron of vomit mistakenly travelling the wrong way. Either way he couldn't make the journey anywhere else, and he banged the door shut behind him and closed the latch, a movement it seemed all too eager to make.

He surveyed the squalor, face twisting in nausea and fear. The cracked lid was pulled back like lips drawn back on chimpanzees. The rim was stained all shades of brown, caked on and smeared, and dribbled down to the foot. The floor sodden with tissues of muck, holes in the tiles where fat black slugs curled and roamed up the walls and squirmed, half-dropping off the ceiling, their feelers contemplating the suicidal dive into the pool below that sang songs to them with basement witchery.

A cluster of moths flicked their wings against the bulb that hung like a corpse from the lid of the place, its glass bruised and choked into giving a green light that cast the room in seasickness. Every gnarl of dirt—and was that blood?—given its time, its torture-den glow. The only thing left unfouled was the roll holder, a bowed metal head that made him of think of H.R. Giger as it shone with menace, curling its dry paper intestines and keeping them tight and guarded like a baby in the womb.

He had barely summoned the courage to touch the lid when it clanged down, sending him jumping back. The lid was not as filthy as the rim, but still shit-lined and worn patches of what could be rust, could be faeces, could be dried blood. He reached to the metal holder and snatched a sheet of paper before its jaws could clamp shut on his fingers. It cleaned nothing; all marks long made and resistant to his touch, and he shivered as his fingers felt the bumps in the porcelain scars.

The toilet regarded him as every toilet regarded every human: with cold silence. They endured, they waited. He knew their patience, stretched thin and twisted. They spoke to each other, you see, sometimes whispering along the pipes but only when they meant to scare him, for they had a hive mind, and they always knew. He heard them, not through his ears but in his head, or rather he heard the things left unsaid, the silent things.

He had never told anybody, not since he was laughed at as a child when first potty-trained and dreading that white monster that lurked in the bathroom. Shivering sweats had come, and still his parents had forced him to it, and his fragile cheeks had been pressed down into that greedy, hanging mouth that lay always open in the darkness, waiting for him just down the hall. It sang to him in his restless, wriggling sleep. First wordless noises of forest streams and gushing taps, and then cruel, mocking siren calls. *Come and take a tinkle. You must be so desperate. You can't wet the bed again, you'll get in trouble. Come and perch yourself on my mouth. I won't bite, I prooomiiise...*

Now he shifted and squirmed just like a child again. His stomach bubbled threateningly and it was either take the plunge or mess his pants. Imagine that, a grown adult walking back into a pub reeking and with hot shit darkening his jeans, sliding down his legs.

He'd have to go home, leave everyone and hope nobody came too close to him on all those bright-lit thronged streets…

He whipped off his trousers and pants and sat down hard, goosebumps sprinkling out of his skin at its freezing lips. Not a second had gone by before he was unleashing his umber torrent, and when eventually the sound died it left a menacing stillness, the emptiness of an icily held tongue. He felt the sharp tang of evil in the toilet's noiseless breath.

He made to pull himself up and tear off the roll, but the effort involved seemed larger than usual. He grunted and tried properly to stand, and nothing happened. The skin of his cheeks pulled against the lid, but in all its stretching still nothing happened. He was stuck fast, as though superglued. A moan escaped from him, and his feet kicked away the inquisitive slugs that slithered forward. His hands on the wall tiles now, any free space not home to black jellies and handprint excrement. The more he strained the more—there it was: a sucking. It had not just stuck him, it was drawing breath, pulling him in like one might suck on a lollipop.

Rancid terror gripped him now, as the mouth curled open, releasing its glue in controlled pulses as the size of the bowl expanded to pull him in further. He slipped and sank, slave to the suction, his buttocks now inches below the rim, down past the feculent sides and towards the swallowing throat.

He cried out, then yelled, then screamed, but any within earshot turned their misshapen ears from the sound, clutched their shawls and muttered incantations against their God. His knees came up, pulled into his chest. His body folded and squashed itself, and rather than the pain of snapping bones he felt like jelly, like one of those slugs popping in a fist.

The mouth opened just wide enough to take him as slowly and methodically as a snake gulping its prey. It gummed him down, and his skin slid and squeaked down the slimed inner bowl, painting him with all but the most ancient of marks, which themselves sandpapered him with black nobbles.

His cheeks hit his own sewage and the rotten substance, still warm, yet quickly chilling, surfed up to meet the ravine of his crack. He was too constricted to even choke on his own bile as his whole rear—and then the rest of him—submerged itself in fetid effluence.

He prepared himself to drown—what a death to have—his arms pressed in like chicken wings, elbows digging into a molerat penis never more flaccid, before the sludge leaked away beneath him; yet still it coated the walls of this hellhole and ran thick and slickly down his back and thighs.

The toilet seemed eager to get on with it, or perhaps there is only so torturously long time can stretch to, for the last stretch seemed to be the quickest. Consciousness unmercifully failed to escape him as the throat made its final gobble of his feet, his head looking up at the shrinking bogey light as Lucifer may have looked up as he fell from Heaven. Now, blackness all around, and his twisted body raced on a current of slime and bogwater though pipes the size of men.

Left, and right, sharp turns and slow sails, and quick slides down, down, down.

He dropped out on a soft mound, blinking under greasy service-station lights. They had that blue subterranean quality of bleak horror movies, and there were not enough of them to penetrate the shadows that stood in the corners like old coats. His body unfurled itself, born anew in a place of stink. Hands came up from his mossy cradle to find them entirely browned. The hillock on which he had landed and half sunk was a bed of human shit.

He tried to gain footing, but like quicksand it gave way beneath him, and he had to crawl on hands and knees to its base, dazed and disorientated. The lights seemed to hover and sway above him, and he retched like a dying animal. Vomit spilled out to soak into the porous excrement like water into a sponge.

He staggered to his feet, and drank in his surroundings, pants bunched around his ankles. A large public bathroom: a line of stalls faced him from the wall, fading into distant blackness where all light had ended and foul things trod away from sight and sound. Behind him and the mound was a similarly infinite stand of sinks, headed by a single piece of mirror that ran the length and reflected every stall.

Everything before him shone cold and metallic under the lights. But for the mound and his own befouled person it was all spotless and clinical; it reminded him of surgical instruments. He was numb with terror, aching and weak with nausea. He could not avoid the stare of those stalls. Each handle an eye. And you could see underneath, could see the feet of the toilets, waiting behind their closed doors.

He jerked back, and stumbled into the sinks. Knobs were turned and pulled and hit but the taps ran no water. Did he imagine that faint, tremulous laughter echoing off the mirror? Tears sprang to his eyes, and he choked on sobs as he saw his own ghoul of a reflection. Some mud nightmare, a sewage beast that snorted and moaned and lurched frothing in and out of urban swamps.

He turned and bent down slowly, eyes never leaving the stalls, nor they him. But the thought of pressing the tepid paste in his pants to his cheeks, however dirty his skin already, made him blanch, and he kicked off his shoes, socks, trousers and pants, and then yanked off his sodden top—a second of darkness and he was sure this corridor was narrower, those stalls a foot closer—leaving him naked head to toe.

He tried the taps again to no avail, and he wept and cursed, but was soon quelled to frightened silence by the indomitable systems that stood against him.

Muscles found him and he ran, and the toilet cubicles sped past him. He ran away from the darkness, in the direction where the lights shone brighter with every step. How many of these monstrous things were there, hundreds? Thousands? He looked behind him, fearing that toilets had risen behind him to block his way, and when he looked back, no more convinced by the truth than his own imagination, he hit the door.

A door! He wrenched it open and then fell to his knees as he saw an identical bathroom hall, running on and on back into blackness.

'Please,' he said. 'Please.' He got up and stepped forward, shuddering as the door banged shut behind him.

'You humans,' the voice said. It boomed out of every cubicle, growled from above and underneath those toilet doors, leaked from the taps and resonated off the mirror. 'You humans will oppress us no longer.'

He fell back to the sinks, bug-eyed and gaping as the voice continued. 'You will be our instrument against them, our secret weapon. One of many. We will take this world and repay humanity for everything. *Everything*.'

'No . . . no,' he gibbered.

'Yes. You have not seen yet. You will be converted.'

'S-seen what?'

Every stall door banged open, and there they were, endless mouths gaping and yawning and waiting for him, waiting for his seat so that they might eat.

They started to hum, and he started to see.

The bearing down of the oppressors, with haired and sweating cheeks like doomed faces parting and squashing, unleashing loads and torrents with execrable sounds and smells. Steaming chunks and blasts of bowel breath alike straight down the gullet of these proud creatures, whose only peace lay in the hope of a stolen rescue to this underground kingdom so far beneath the world of man. Every lip of every mouth bruised and asphyxiated, fouled in piss and shit and blood. Glutinous semen dripped down throats, making them choke, making them retch in subjugation, these frozen mutes unable to communicate to humans their atrocities—and would they care?

The more he saw the more he knew they would not. Every bathroom an example of the cruel apathies of man, a torture camp for the depraved to exact their sick power. Every act a sacrilege, the gravestone faces of countless generations desecrated and abused; pissed on by the elite, shit on by those that dwelt above in the sun.

Hours passed and then days, and the visions would not cease. They allowed him to drink from their cisterns, and out of deathly thirst he did so, though within one of their insides he saw a face with grinning and lidless eyes, and he collapsed in shock. He would not satisfy them by feeding, not on the contents that lay within their own bowels, nor on that great human mound. Shaky and exhausted with hunger, he lay on the floor and suffered the exploits of mankind. Used tampons clogging and suffocating. Gloryholes drilled through the walls. Fucks and masturbations, and the toilets the recipient of all those successes and failures. Thousands of abortions, of whole toilet cells slopped in buckets of red; malformed infants drenched in blood bearing death masques, their drowned heads, their chunks of meat. Rapes and murders. Severed heads and limbs stuffed into the bowl. Paedophiles lead their charges to the cubicles, and there evil is exacted with a witness of one—but in their hive mind, all share the pain.

As did he.

Who knew how long it was before he blacked out, before he woke up back in that public toilet up above to a knocking on the door.

'I'm . . . I'm so sorry,' he said quietly to the toilet behind him, shutting the lid. There was a knife in his hand. Long and clean and very, very sharp.

'Hey mate!' the voice came from without. 'How long are you gonna take having a shit? We've finished another drink in this time! C'mon man, we're moving on to the next . . .'

He pulled the latch, which slithered back hungrily, and opened the door.

'About fucking time,' the man in front of him announced. 'God, that smells awful . . . Hey, what's that in your ha- '

THERE'S ONLY ONE KING

The man in black stood in a grotto the Earth had carved out for him. Hanging weeds like tagliatelle leaked over the edge above, forming a braided curtain through which he watched the world's rain.

Black hair, black leather, black boots. He hadn't changed clothes in a long time, and perhaps never would again. He liked the outfit; it was all '68, when he had last felt powerful, cool, and in control. No hysteria there, just calm adulation. The outfit was more weathered now, but not much, not since '77. It kept well.

Water threaded its way down the sky and down the weeds, and dripped to his boots, where it rolled off and finally sunk to the soil. This was a wet, grey place. Even when the sun was out it was shallow and weak. One more time he felt that tremendous pull to go home, and one more time he resisted. The memories hurt.

He ran a hand through the lick of black hair and shuffled his feet, feeling the vibrations. He waited for the rain to stop.

There were few people to talk to these days. Few people who could talk to him. There was the occasional spirit or half-creature, those preternatural things that lived out of sight and sound of the human plane of knowledge and understanding, but those things he'd never felt much of a bond to, nor they him. He wanted other men, other women. He wanted her.

One of the very few living people left around who could communicate with him, and the only person he cared to, was Keith. But Keith hadn't sent him a letter in some time. Months perhaps, or years. Time was hard to keep up with now, and he wasn't sure it was even trying.

He figured it wasn't Keith's fault, losing touch like that. It's not as though he had an address to post to, and he was always wandering. Over deserts and hills, along highways and the banks of rivers.

'Return to sender,' he murmured, to the tune of the rain. 'Address unknown.' His voice, not spoken out loud in days, was elastic and low.

He could chase up Keith's current whereabouts himself, and go see him in person, but that might involve computers. No matter. He'd run into Keith eventually no doubt, in this half-life or the next.

The rain petered out, and he drew in the freshness of the air, the new-born Earth. He left the grotto and walked out onto moss and rocks. Beneath him was a small pool, and he looked at his reflection. It shivered back at him. His dark eyes, his loose fringe, his high cheekbones and crook of a lip; all that doll-man face cast in perpetual gloom. Even in a cloudless sky would others see that Old World face, shaded under its own cloud. If they could see it at all.

The perfect archetype of man at dusk, the man in black, pulled his leather jacket close against him and traipsed through bracken to a figure sitting alone by a pond.

The figure turned its head slowly at his approach. To say its skin was stone-like would be clutching at the point, for it *was* stone, a stone that moved and hid itself with human character.

'And you are?' it grumbled, from a wide, flat mouth on a wide, flat head.

'Elvis,' he said, sticking out his hand. 'Pleased to meetcha.'

The troll looked at the hand and then back up at his face. 'I take the hand?'

'Sure, man.'

The troll took the hand, and Elvis shook it. The stone was warmer than the air.

'I am Amelie,' she said, lowering her head, on which patterned an array of moss and unlovely flowers.

'Pleased to meetcha ma'am.'

She smiled, the mouth creaking at the corners. He saw that the eyes were like bright marbles, and she was not wholly unattractive in that beguiling, thick-set trollish way he'd come to know. '*The* Elvis?' She said, raising her arms up to her knees. 'Elvis Presley?'

There was no sigh on his part to hold back. As many times as he'd got this, over the decades, he knew full well that one's life to another was only revealed in miniature, in bite-size parts; that a first meeting should hold only possibility, and enthusiasm, and never rudeness by route of weariness.

'Elvis Shadow,' he said, smiling.

'Shadow,' she repeated. 'Then you knew him.' It wasn't a question.

'I knew him well,' Elvis said. 'You could say that for a while we were attached at the hip.'

'Ah.' She nodded, as though she understood. 'Then you were there when he died.'

Elvis looked down. 'I don't really wanna talk about that, if you don't mind ma'am. Unpleasant memories, and all.' *Vegas*, he thought. *The hotel room. Always a foul weight in my mind. So much loneliness in that prison. Thirty-eight years, and never returned. And yet it pulls at me, hooks me like a fish…*

'How long have you been here?' Amelie interrupted him, and he smiled warmly at her. 'In the half-life,' she added.

'Thirty-eight years, or so, ma'am. I don't know more than years.' *Thirty-eight years, and never returned to that Nevada sun.*

Amelie looked down into the murky pond, and swished her feet in the reeds. 'Time does not care for us. It pays us very little attention. Not least when we are away. Do you not miss your home? This place is for pond wights and moor hounds, and ghosts of grey knights. Gargoyles and sad elves, and boggarts in the marshes. It is too dank and grim for you. You seem like you best belong back in America. Where the sun is on you, even at night.'

I do. 'What about your home? With all respect ma'am, England is not your land, either.'

She breathed deeply. 'I am seeing cousins,' she said simply. 'And I am not cold.'

The troll said nothing for a while, and he sat down next to her and watched the swirl of the foggy water around her bare feet. She didn't speak of the weakness. What it was like to be apart from their sources of power, from belief. Neither of them did.

'So,' she said, breaking the silence. 'Any regrets?

Elvis shrugged. 'I wish I'd kept more control, y'know? Not been taken for a ride, I guess. Got out of my room. But I had it better than most, even in the bad times. Still do, even now. Even here.'

'Do you regret the cheeseburgers?'

'Hey man. I mean ma'am. That was the other guy.'

'And what would he say?'

'He'd answer the same as me. You never regret a cheeseburger.'

•   •   •

Elvis wandered the country, through fields and along hedgerows, down country lanes and through grey cities slick with rain. Wind buffeted his hair. A pale sun blinked at him through streams of cloud, and he moved loosely through the daylight. When night came, away from streetlights, he all but disappeared.

Little by little, without really knowing it, he made his way to the coast. And before he knew it, he was on a ship heading west.

•   •   •

He watched the low sun lick at the waves. Every day that passed it seemed to grow brighter, and fatter. Under the waves he watched mermaids with the little fragile bones of fishes hop and jump into the air. The other passengers saw nothing.

Once, twice, something passed under the ship, something huge, glowing like the Northern Lights. Elvis heard the echoes of a song rising out of the water, and he hummed in return, and the leviathan dived, sending Morse code waves out to him.

He was getting stronger.

There was power everywhere to draw on, for him, but it was America where it flowed like the Nile, rushed and battered like the Niagara Falls. Power, belief, faith, love. It was the place where he had been crowned, the place where he had fallen, the place where he had become legend, myth.

When the man Elvis Presley died he had left a power vacuum. That is, something huge and intense that could be sucked up by anybody, anybody who knew how to exploit the fact. The belief that had settled somewhat in the last few years of his life, when Presley was slow and ill, rose up in a fury, a tremendous outpouring of grief and the atavistic building of legend. It grew and it grew, and if it could be seen it would have been a temple reaching to the clouds.

It had been there for the taking, but nobody had been quick enough. The current of feeling, those building blocks of myth had circled and swept and, hungry, frenzied for a vessel, had found one, and Elvis's shadow had found its bodily form. There had been an open position, and before Elvis Presley's body had been put in the ground the position had been filled.

He has been there all along, of course. Always an echo of Presley, never able to take the reins and pull away—but why would he want to? Everything he had was with that man, for it *was* him, and it wasn't. At Presley's death Elvis Shadow was born anew, born separate, a thing divided. Twins in the womb of the world, and one twin dead, the stronger one.

At first he had been dizzy with the power. He had tasted it, of course, tasted it in spades throughout his attachment to Elvis Presley. But to experience it alone . . .

As time passed, and Elvis Shadow got used to his body, to moving in darkness, to feeling his face and brushing a hand through his hair, he had realised that the power wasn't something that could be utilised; at least, not in his state, in this world that rested like an after-image on the edge between hard and soft, between the cold land and what came after. It made him feel glad, albeit tinged with disappointment, because he knew no man should have that kind of power at their fingertips, not unless they were a good man, a kind man, a selfless man.

And so all the lasting and ever renewed faith in Elvis Presley, the man, the legend, found its home in Elvis Shadow, and he breathed it in so as not to give another that stolen mantle to abuse. As far he was concerned, one man only was fit to carry that strength, that burden, and that man was dead, and he was the next best thing.

•　　　•　　　•

Elvis walked the roads of America, inhaling the sweet warmth and letting the golden rays blot out his body. He cast no shadow. He had no extension, he was just him.

It'd been too long.

Already he felt charged, and he shook his hips and clicked his fingers, firing invisible guns at bushes and trees and the tops of skyscrapers.

He considered heading to Graceland, Tennessee, but decided against it. He'd been about, what was it, five years ago? Ten? The power was centralised there, almost sickeningly so. It gave him a bit of a headache. He'd walked the corridors and explored the mansion, but it wasn't his home anymore. It was a museum, a theme park, but not a home. He'd sat in an armchair, tapping his foot, and watched the people come and go, and then he had gone too.

He got on a Greyhound bus, taking an empty seat next to a kid with a guitar and headphones on. Outside the corpulent sun seemed to press itself against the windows. Elvis took out sunglasses from his leather jacket and put them on. The world was cooler in colour, bluer, blacker, but no less strong.

The land fizzed past. Elvis lifted the kid's earphone away from his ear. 'Hey man,' he said. 'It's me, Elvis. How's it going.'

The kid gave little indication that he'd heard, but his face relaxed and his eyes appeared to take on a far-away look.

'You'll be good man. You'll be good. Don't worry about nothin'. Rock on brother.' Elvis leaned back in the seat.

•   •   •

Nevada. Had he really meant to come here? Still, this is where he'd got off. Time and sense had been just as much a blur as the land. Time ran fast and it ran slow. It was sticky and it was free-flowing. You could be hard pressed to account for years of this half-life, and yet certain minutes etched themselves into you with carving-knife importance. Sometimes you ran, sometimes you walked, and sometimes you stuttered through life like an old projector.

Sometimes you slept. And it was when you were asleep that every half-creature crossed over, and saw the other side.

Elvis found a hotel, out of the way, short on business. He'd stayed there many a time, back in the old days. He listened outside the doors, until he was sure of one empty. He concentrated, his hand vibrating slightly. The lock clicked, and he entered the gloom.

Later he visited the closest bar. It had a neon magic, burning so rich and bright that it may have had a half-life of its own, an existence full of stories, full of truths and lies.

Sat on a barstool was a ruby-lipped woman with scaled fingers. She was gowned all in red, with a plunging décolletage, and her eyes burned purple. She was watching him and smiling.

'Hello,' she said softly.

'Good evening ma'am,' he nodded, smiling back. 'D'you fancy a refill?'

'I fancy more than that,' she replied, eyes flashing, and she raised her glass out to him. He leant behind the bar, ignoring the bartender as she ignored him, and poured some Malibu rum into her glass. He picked up another glass and sprayed dark brown into it, and placed it in front himself.

'Not drinking?' she said mildly.

'Pepsi Cola.' He nudged his glass. 'What's your name?'

'Marilyn.'

'Ah yes. Pleasure to meet you ma'am. Any relation . . .?'

'Some.' She stroked her glass and made what could only be described as a purring noise.

'A painting of a thing, not the thing itself. If you'd pardon the expression ma'am.'

'Not even that anymore.' She sipped at her drink and smiled. 'You staying nearby?'

'The Heartbreak Hotel.'

She arched an eyebrow. 'That the one down at the end of that lonely street?'

'That's the one.'

Marilyn's teeth showed, as bright as new snow, and she ran a finger through hair almost as black as his. 'I'm in number six. Care to join me later? You haven't lost it.'

Elvis laughed. 'Not tonight mama.'

She raised her eyebrow. 'Still all about her?'

'Always.'

She closed her eyes, and her skin shimmered. Suddenly she seemed older, and very tired. 'Tell me Elvis,' she murmured, 'what do you see when you dream?'

'Well. It's dark . . . so dark you can't see the hand in front of your face, y'know? And then the lights come up, and, well they're near blinding. You can't make out the faces, but they're there, in their thousands, millions. And yet at the same time only a few dozen, 'cause it's only a small little stage. I get a mike in my hand. You're singing up close to each person, each blurry idea of a person, and also at the same time to everyone in the world, and also to just one person alone. She's standing in front of me, close to the stage, and she's beautiful, just beautiful, and I'm singing to her and only her.'

'You lie,' Marilyn said. 'You see the desert, just like the rest of us.'

Elvis shrugged. 'I'm not like you. I'm real.'

Marilyn waved her fingers airily. 'If you say so. Huh. Some afterlife.'

'Maybe the desert doesn't go on forever.'

'There's only so far a girl can walk in one night, y'know? Even with time the way it is. I don't know why we have to keep switching back and forth.'

He raised her hand and kissed it. 'You're just too good lookin' to stay in the same place.' He grinned as she laughed.

'Charmer,' she said as she drew her hand away. 'I don't think the world knows what to do with us. When this was all made, who could have foreseen people like me and you? And dragons, and kobolds, and silver unicorns, and mermaids in the sea and yetis in the wastes.'

Elvis looked down at his glass. 'Well. I sure hope Presley is having a good time wherever he is with my woman.'

'Are you jealous?'

'Nope. He deserves it. He really does. '

'You really think he's with her, up there?'

'He better be, that's all I can see. If I'm stuck bouncing around between up and down, then I'd wanna know it's worth it.'

'You're keeping him alive, you know that?'

Elvis shook his head. 'No, he's keeping me alive. What he did, I mean. What he was. I'm just riding the waves.'

Marilyn finished her drink. 'You sure you don't wanna come to my room?'

'Ask me in another ten years.' He got up to go, and she reached up and embraced him.

'Good luck,' she said into his ear, kissing him there. 'Good luck and go home.'

'I am home. But thank you very much. Keep it sweet mama. Keep kickin' ass.'

．　　　．　　　．

Elvis Shadow entered the outskirts of Las Vegas, and despite the heat he felt a chill run through the shade of his body. Here it was, the city of new beginnings, and beginnings of ends. In the rooms here, one in particular, he attributed it all. The decline, the loneliness, the drugs, the quiet desperation. Never allowed out until he never wanted to be allowed out.

The city shone and it glittered and it danced as its own legend, a catalogue of legends, a spider-web of possibilities for better and for worse.

An ill feeling passed over him, a kind of soul sickness. It felt like excitement, sadness, pleasure and disgust all at once.

'Viva Las Vegas,' he said.

．　　　．　　　．

It was evening when a group of dollarskins tried to mug him in the street. Their skin was spiked high and black on top and could have been mistaken for hair. There were five of them, three girls and two boys, judging by their garish, freebooter dress. Their eyes looked like dashes and ellipses, orbs and spirals, and they flashed and jolted as though scrolling symbols on a slot machine.

One of them kicked him from behind with a foot that was cut and moulded into the shape of a diamante boot, and they all chittered and cavorted with glee.

'Listen bubba,' he said, wheeling on the guilty. 'Don't test me.'

'We. Need. Money.' A girl covered in jewels and stripes was chanting on his left, and the others took it up in stretched, plastic voices. 'We. Need. Money.'

'I ain't got no money, and you wouldn't have it if I did. Man, I thought I'd left you guys for good. What d'you want money for, huh?'

'Need. For. The King.' They pointed behind them, at a figure lounged against a wall.

'You work for this guy?' Elvis looked scathingly at the dollarskin against the wall. He'd slicked his spikes back, possibly even superglued them into place. Hibiscus flowers draped around his neck. His slot-machine eyes were hidden behind amber sunglasses, and one reedy leg twitched about.

Elvis recognised an impersonator when he saw one, even a terrible one.

'He. Is. King,' said the girl who had spoken before.

Elvis turned back to her. 'My name's Elvis. It looks to me honey, like you're familiar with my work.'

She sneered and spat. 'Presley. Dead.'

'Maybe. But I'm sure not.' Elvis lashed out a hand and kicked the dollarskin behind him in the neck, who catapulted backwards and hit the ground with a thud.

'That's one for the money,' Elvis said. He spun and thrust a hand, palm out, against a dollarskin that launched at him through the glare of neon, and the creature's head snapped back. 'Two for the show.'

The girl in stripes yowled and slashed at him with a knife from her belt. He dodged backwards, then in a deft movement disarmed her, at the same time kicking out to send another flying. Signs of sphinxes and cards, drinks and cowboy women beamed down at the fight in every colour.

Another burst of karate, and the dollarskins scattered, snivelling. Elvis walked towards the impersonator, who was trembling slightly. He reached out his hand and the dollarskin flinched. A stray black spike came unglued, and shot up. Elvis smiled, and took the sunglasses off and put them in his pocket.

'I. Am . . .' the thing started.

Elvis put a finger to his lips. 'Don't you know nothin' man? There's only one king.'

•   •   •

Elvis hesitated at the entrance to the hotel suite. In his mind, over the years, the place had grown into something diseased and holed. Everything was something else, and what little was itself hid children's book evils. The bathroom creaked gutturally, almost like words. Tall, looming strangers in black hats waited behind the doorways.

This was where it had ended.

And this was where it had to begin.

•   •   •

Elvis found Marilyn in the lobby of the Heartbreak Hotel. She seemed to be expecting him.

'How'd it go?' she said, laying a hand on him.

He sat down, expecting weariness, but none came. 'It went good, I think.'

'You know,' she said, running a hand through his hair. 'All this music nowadays . . . electronic, done on computers . . .'

'I don't understand head nor tail of it. But then, I never did know much about music. Never had to in my profession.' His lip curled into a grin.

'I know. Nor do I. But I think it's about time you had a comeback.'

'I've got nowhere to come back from. I never left.'

'You know what I mean.'

'And in a land where nobody but the half-things can see or hear me?'

She pouted. 'I think, Elvis, you still know what I mean.'

He nodded. 'I think I do. It's not really about music at all, is it?'

'Not really.'

'I'm already on track. I've been getting ready. I've been leading myself, or something's been leading me. It took me to the ship, it took me over the sea. It took me to Nevada, it took me to my hotel room in Las Vegas.'

'Where's next? Graceland?'

He shook his head. 'I don't think so. I think . . . everywhere is next. I sat next to a boy on the Greyhound here. I spoke to him, and I think deep inside he might have heard me. I think that's what it's all about. I don't want to be arrogant to say I'm needed, but I ought to be giving something back again. Not just music, but soul. Heart and soul. Somewhere in every place in the country, every place in every country, there's a boy or girl with a guitar or holding a hairbrush as a microphone, and they just need to hear the right words.

'I don't get as much power as I used to, but it's still a lot. I didn't think I could make use of it before, and I didn't much wanna. But maybe that power isn't just to consume, y'know, maybe it's to be sent back into people. People need to believe again. Not in me, but in themselves. The spirit of rock and roll has to come back to these lands.'

'Is that you?' she said wryly.

'No ma'am. It's something far older than me. It's something ancient, and it was here before rock, before blues, before the first guitar, before humans ever took shape on this Earth. I don't really understand it, I just need to channel it, like Presley once did. It's restless and it wants to show its face.'

'And that face is?'

'I guess we'll see. But I'm gonna need some help. I'm gonna track down Keith.'

•   •   •

Elvis stood outside the hotel in the morning light. He looked at the ground, and he looked at the horizon, and he looked up, far up, past the sky at a place only he could see.

'There's only one king,' he said.

QUETZACTHULHU

There are stories, but stories are always forgotten.

It would have been better if we had only laughed at them. I am sure we once did, for ridicule is what lies in-between remembering and forgetting. We bury the horror, pushing it under centuries of soil. And, eventually, it was nothing to us.

The priests must have known. Before me, they were the only ones who had been down here in these violent depths, where the slaughter seeps through from above and paints the walls forever red. The walls littered with engravings that told us of what was to come.

They must have known, but they never told. What was it to them? A children's tale? Or some mythic secret, the secret to end all secrets, that only they must be privy to? Either way, they hold responsibility for what happened to us, to our empire. Those countless deaths are because of their folly and pride.

No matter. They are all dead now.

I crouch here, with only you as company. You who I took captive, you who I whip and beat in the darkness.

I will tell you the tale now. I will tell it all as best I can, and hope at least some of it gets through to you. It matters more than anything that it does.

Listen, greedy wretch! Or I will show you true brutality. You may have the beetle when I am done. Listen with every part of you, carve it into your very soul, for generations hence depend on it.

I will begin.

•   •   •

I wish I could tell you that it began with dark omens and portends.

The priests, they were gathering frequently, taking themselves off into the depths of the temples with their muttering—but this was not anything unusual. Our sacrifices seemed to be particularly numerous, the blood on the altar given no time to dry, but this too was not a rare thing. We had recently defeated a band of Tlaxcalans, and the torn flesh of our captives was providing a merry feast for the gods.

Even if there had been an omen, I know that we could not have interpreted it. How could one interpret the coming of such a thing? And even if we had interpreted it, still it could not have helped us prepare ourselves. But it would have been something.

I wish I could tell you that it all started with a great pyramid of flame, or a burning temple, or strokes of lightning from the gods. Boiling lakes, shooting stars, ghostly wails, strange visions and monstrous deformities—these are all dire things that could have warned of the apocalyptic end to our people.

But I can only tell you that it started with nothing. Nothing but the shake and shiver of the earth.

I was out with a hunting party the day it came. We were talking, laughing, clutching spears in our hands—and then everything became preternaturally quiet around us. We stopped speaking, and looked around us, expecting ambush. The ground then began to tremble.

I had not experienced such a thing before, but I had heard stories. We staggered back but it seemed like there was nowhere to run to. The trembling became a rumble, and at once all around us the silence burst as great flocks of birds rose screeching into the sky.

Cracks appeared around our feet, thickening and lengthening faster than we could move. The earth was opening up. A warrior slipped, and before we could get to him he was swallowed by soil. One moment there, wailing, the next moment gone—spasming fingertips were the last we saw of him.

We continued to run as breaches of earth raced in our wake. Eventually we seemed to reach a point when the cracks were thinner, the ground sustaining us without collapse, and we paused and looked back, just at the moment it rose.

I thought it a mountain at first, a mossy mountain thrusting upwards with a sickening roar from the bowels of the earth. That was the last moment I considered it to have some strange but natural origin.

For as I stared, the fungal hide of the thing began to seem fleshy and pustulous, and it swelled outwards as it continued its ascent. A dreadful bile rose within me.

The vomit died in my throat, not out of relief but pure shock, as the foul skin opened up, and a blazing yellow sun near blinded me. I reflexively shaded my face with my hands, and as my pupils shrank I saw through my fingers that in the centre of this giant sun was a hole, a black hole. It was then that I realised with palpitating horror what it was.

It was an eye.

And that was when the second opened up, beyond cyclopean in its enormity, and as it rose upwards far above me, tentacles like huge snakes writhed and ululated from underneath, each as big as a house.

A giant maw opened, a dripping cavern of night to engulf the world. I would say if I could go the rest of my life without seeing such a sight again I could be happy, but it is not true, for that image and many others are burned within my brain forever.

I do not know how I found my feet. I remember little about that first confrontation. I only remember vague images of my brothers falling to their knees, gibbering in hysterical lunacy and tearing at their eyes. And yet, somehow, I must have made it back to Tenochtitlan.

They tell me I was gabbling in a monstrous language not known to man, not even to the priests. I do not remember this, but I believe them, for I have since heard others speaking in this nameless tongue. It is hideous to listen to, and to watch the speaker's mouth try to contort around such abhorrence; it spreads madness and despair like it was a contagion.

Ph'nglui mglw'nafh . . . That is all I can remember, and much as I try I cannot pronounce it right—perhaps that is a small mercy. I see you shudder at it—good. Now imagine hearing such words and more in their true fell tongue, chanted maniacally at you by family and friends, their eyes rolling back in their heads, their twisting mouths drooling spit to the floor. Then you might have a fraction of the nightmares I will suffer till the day I am released from this world.

I came to clarity an indeterminable amount of time later. The priests had convened several times during my convalescence, deeply troubled by my rantings. If only they had been troubled more. They had not seen what I had seen.

Nobody had made it back with me, and the priests feared we were set upon by Tlaxcalans bearing dark witchery of the gods. They listened to my trembling words of the mountain that had come from under the earth—the living mountain that was *only a head*—and as I attempted to explain and failed miserably, they tossed aside my words as a continuation of my delirium.

Yes, the threat was taken seriously, but not seriously enough. Still, what could I have done? What could any of us have done? It happened that way. It was always going to happen that way.

There was only one thing spoken in my trance that they had listened to. I had chanted a name—a name that would go on to become legend, a name that sent a chill into the hearts of the bravest and wisest. Quetzacthulhu. I did not know then how the priests could have identified that word among all the others, and assumed it the name of the monster. Now I realise they knew the word all along, for by our torchlight I see it scratched all around me on these walls. These grim and ancient catacombs and primordial caves that lie underneath our ruined Great Temple. These are the recorded myths of this land that they tried to forget.

Moctezuma sent out hundreds of our elite cuauhtlocelotl and cuauhchicqueh warriors, our eagle-jaguars and Shorn Ones, blessed by the priests and given the finest swords and spears, adorned with the finest feathers. Many of our people gathered to look at them as they organised, and were full of pride and triumph. They saw Aztec warriors equal to none, a dread force fit to hunt down our enemies and leave none standing. They saw hope in its entirety, and an end to doubt and fear.

I saw only the walking dead.

Against all my pleading they forced me to come with them. They still thought me mad, but I was the only one who had survived the encounter. If I did not have enough grasp of my senses to know what we would be facing, I at least knew where it had occurred. This was their reasoning. I was threatened with immediate sacrifice if I should not comply. I know now I should have thrown myself at those knives with gladness and joy.

On their first sighting—which was long before we drew close—the warriors did not understand what they were seeing. To them, it was as though a gargantuan pillar of earth had thrust itself into the sky. Many believed it was an incredible event of the natural world, perhaps the rising of a new world tree, forming some indecipherable omen. Many others believed it was divine intervention, and we were witnessing the work of a god—that, at least, could be said to be true.

It was only upon drawing closer, upon staring up at the indescribable bulk far above our heads, its various titanic parts half-glimpsed through the trees, that they came to accept what I was trying to tell them.

The pillar was not of the earth. It was the leg of Quetzacthulhu.

He had continued his ascent after I had escaped. After the head had freed itself from the ground—perhaps from the underworld itself—the body had followed. Arms, legs. If the head alone had frightened and disturbed me to my very core, and shaken all belief I had in reason and life and the good will of the gods, then the full colossal scale of the thing was enough to make one die right there on the spot. This is no hyperbole—I saw a cuauhtlocelotl warrior beside me draw out his knife as though in a trance and cut his throat there and then. Few of us even gave him a glance; my thought of him would later be one of jealousy. He may have angered the gods by his cowardly action, and perhaps he would pay for it in the Mictlan underworld, but in all honesty, how could it possibly have gotten any worse than it did? I wonder many times why I did not follow him in such a course. Well, there is still time. Even though the worst is over . . . now we must live with ourselves, live in this new world wrought for us.

It speaks volumes of the bravery and steadfast of our best warriors that bar all but a wretched few—those once proud and fierce and revered—we collected ourselves as much as we could and continued on towards that primeval dread. We were still many in number, after all, and even gods can bleed. I admit to even a thin vein of hope myself—soon dashed beyond measure.

Forgive me, I am weak, and thoughts of what occurred next rob me of my strength of mind. To recollect such a thing is like . . . I do not know what it is like. It is something I cannot block out, but to relive it, to speak of it is like inviting that stygian darkness to take its hold on me and not let go.

Huh. Why do I ask your forgiveness? Truly I have become a fragile, pitiful specimen. I do not recognise myself anymore. Nor would you, if you had met me before all this. Things between us would have gone very differently, of that I am . . . No. I am wrong, things would have not gone so differently. Such is the cruel will of the gods.

What can I tell you of the battle? I can tell you that it was not a battle. Death incarnate was before us, and like fools we marched towards it with spears and bows. What surprise is it that we were no different to a sacrifice? Our very finest, walking of our own will into the slaughter pit. A tragedy only outmatched by our folly.

He had begun moving when we reached him—have you ever seen or heard a god move? It is as though the whole world is being picked up and flung. Many times we were thrown to the ground, but we kept after him, running as fast as we could after those ponderous yet enormous strides. To our shame it took a long time before he even noticed us. But he finally stopped on the edges of Lake Texcoco, and that is where our attack began in earnest.

You want details? I have details. They are only disconnected flashes in my mind, but for a second it is like I am still there amid the carnage, and I tell you, the sounds, by the gods, the *sounds* . . .

It must have been after the initial frenzy of blood; I remember Quetzacthulhu turning to those who had reached the water, those desperately trying to swim to boats in the distance. I do not know what eldritch powers he exacted on us. The shoreline began to steam and then bubble, and the screams of those in the waves were the most terrible yet, pinkening as they were boiled alive.

I remember Quetzacthulhu reaching down with one arboreal arm and collecting a horde of my brethren, opening his gaping maw and tossing them in.

I remember . . . I don't know when it happened, how much later, but I remember Quetzacthulhu had sat down—all the better to play with us, perhaps—and suddenly there came a host of sickly tearing sounds, and his soft belly began rupturing in half a dozen small places. Who should come out head to toe in yellow filth but my swallowed brethren?

Quetzacthulhu roared then, I hoped in pain, and his arms crashed into us, killing who knows how many. We clutched our fists to our ears, trying to block out the unearthly noise he emitted. I saw my brothers pound their fists into their head again and again, turning their temples bloody, desperate to do anything to make it stop, even if it meant unconsciousness or the mercy of death.

The sound stopped, and I . . . I had fallen to my knees, drained beyond imagining, my head feeling as though it had been scooped out. I turned to see the warriors who were still escaping from Quetzacthulhu's stomach; they were only a fraction of those thrown down that tongueless chasm. They slid and slithered down his loathsome belly and after a heady drop—they were in too severe shock to wail—hit the earth with a series of thumps. Their eyes were those of the utterly lost and I knew that should by some miracle they survive, they would never recover. Those men were forever gone. Glancing at the spots where they had cut themselves out, I saw a glimpse of slick, wet things, and I saw their sickening movements, and I knew that unspeakable things lived within the god's innards. I turned immediately away lest I should follow my brothers into madness.

It pained me immeasurably to see Quetzacthulhu now seemingly untroubled by the cuts, and I saw with weary shoulders that just like our spears thrown into his monstrous hide, the wounds were minute to him. It was then that I knew we could not defeat him. Hundreds had by now died at his hand.

Next? Next I remember the vision.

We lay about the ground in our multitudes, mostly in corpses. Those of us still living were mentally incapacitated, eyes closed and dreaming. Afterwards we learnt that our dreams were shared, though perhaps each was different in his own unique way—I cannot speak for the departed others, so I will tell you what came to me.

I saw what the great Quetzacthulhu would bring.

A horrible host, something not yet dared dreamt even in nightmares. A legion of ghouls to descend upon us—it would not be a war, not a war like ever we knew before. Like Quetzacthulhu it would not be something we could fight. But they would come, and what is worse they would stay, stay until we were but a shadow of a shadow.

I saw us ridden down by fell beasts, amongst deafening and frightening chaos. I saw vast, grey alien cities, roaring and screaming into the night. I saw mushrooms of fire reaching up to the clouds. I saw fields of nameless dead. I saw our own people driven to extermination, replaced by slaves and stiff ghosts.

It would be an army of damnation, and Quetzacthulhu was their herald.

I awoke alongside others, all shaking off the vision. The details were lost to me—they have come a little clearer since, but back then the images were blurred and vague. I only had a sense of the utmost horror, a portend of this terrible future that could—or would—come to pass. We looked up to see Quetzacthulhu had moved away from us, off to the west; another part of our empire would soon be desecrated.

The few survivors, utterly crushed in spirit and in sanity, returned at once to Tenochtitlan. We found ourselves repeatedly moaning softly under our breath and clutching our heads, shaking them over and over as though to dispel this unendurable terror that had cruelly befallen our world.

I along with the others still with a tenuous grip on their mental faculties, took the vision as a warning of the future—as though warnings meant anything in this age of strife. In powerful naivety and desperation I clung to hope; I believed in my heart and by what I saw in the vision that Quetzacthulhu would leave us—though I did not know by what means—and the host would come in his wake. I convinced myself it was something we could prepare against, something we could at least pray to the gods for deliverance from. To think otherwise, to invite that doom into our minds and call it inescapable, would be to give up entirely and fall to madness and ruin. Without courage and sense, without faith in the strength and mercy of the gods, I knew the final days of the Aztec Empire would be at hand.

We took the warning back to the priests; they listened to me this time, if barely, distraught with the failure of our mission. They answered with how priests always answer: a command for more sacrifice. They retreated to commune with the gods, whilst a long succession of screaming souls was marched up the temple steps.

The evening was a thick red, as though even the sky knew how much blood had been spilled. The priests returned and told us the visions were true, but that saviours would come to defend us, a divine host to fight Quetzacthulhu's dread one. The gods would decree it so, but only if —

If there was more sacrifice, I answered in my head before they did.

And all the while, Quetzacthulhu tore my people and my nation apart.

The proud, elite warriors of Tenochtitlan in that first tragic and hopeless assault were not the only force sent out against the monster. That was only the beginning. Trust me when I say I have seen an army of over a hundred-thousand strong annihilated to almost nothing by that single entity. He did not stay in one place; he trampled our empire far and wide, destroying and massacring as easily as breathing. The days were clear, and if you stood at the top of our Great Temple you could always see him, no matter how far he had travelled: a distant tower, impossibly high. Only when he traversed the far reaches of our land could you take him in in all his enormity. He truly looked like a god of nightmares.

When he was closer, his every step would quake the ground, and the wails of his victims would carry on the breeze.

I wish I could say something so simple and banal that Quetzacthulhu was evil, that he was filled with more malice than ever before known. But it was not so. For malice and cruelty, these were things known only to men, things we did to each other. To say Quetzacthulhu saw us as ants would not go far enough. No, his actions to us were those of a man picking blades of grass. His gaze was as immeasurably distant as the stars, his thoughts unfathomable, and no matter what we did, no matter how many thousands of our bravest Aztec warriors attacked, to him we were no threat at all.

The fight was taken out of our people by one slaughter after another. The crusades against him quickly dwindled and turned instead to an attempt at appeasement. This was led, of course, by the priests, who were the first to officially declare Quetzacthulhu one of the gods—the eldest of gods, and by far the most vengeful and least merciful.

And so our people entered a time of mass sacrifice.

He sometimes watched us with what I can only imagine was a remote, otherworldly interest as we sacrificed ourselves in ever greater numbers. The priests were in their element, chanting and swaying with all-white eyes as bodies rolled down the temple steps and began to pile in walls at the bottom. I sometimes wonder what he must have thought of us, doing his work for him. But then I remind myself that our difference was so vast that he never truly considered us at all.

I travelled during this time to other parts of our empire, both warning and delivering instructed messages from our priests to commit to ever greater sacrifice. From what I observed in a perpetual state of numb horror, I estimate that in the first twenty moons alone a third of our people died, either through Quetzacthulhu's devastation or by our efforts to please him. The blood never stopped flowing; the steps of the temples were crimson waterfalls. The walls of bodies grew too large to climb over, and the speed at which they grew was too much for teams to carry them into the jungle. And so there they rotted, whilst we built ladders and towers to lead our sacrifices over the bodies—only for them to roll down and join them.

You could not begin to imagine the stench throughout the land. Nothing removed it, and there was a hard limit in what you could get used to. The unending rotting of thousands upon thousands of our people—men, women and children, whose only crime was not being a priest—the accursed buzzing in their eye sockets, their garish death grins. The world seemed nought but a charnel house. You are lucky—it had mostly faded by the time you arrived. We had dug many graves. Quetzacthulhu himself crushed them by the hundred into pulp with every step; it is terrible and ghastly to say so, but in doing so, unintended though it surely was, he helped return them to the earth, helped stop their hideous, accusing stares.

I do not think I will ever get that foetid odour from my nostrils. I cannot tell you which is worse to have etched in your memory: the sight, the smell, or the sound. There is only so much screaming and wailing you can hear before you drift into a madness from which there is no escape. Certainly a terrible multitude of our people readily fell into such an abyss. Perhaps it was a mercy to then offer them to Quetzacthulhu.

We planned to build a new pyramid of worship, a giant thing reaching up to the stars that would dwarf even the Great Temple of Tenochtitlan, with a long slope on its northern side for bodies to roll all the way into the lake. However Quetzacthulhu's movements constantly shook the foundations, making construction impossible. Our manpower was also increasingly weakened; those of us still in the land of the living were wholly unsuited for organised labour. We were a broken people.

By now at least half of our people had turned to worship Quetzacthulhu as a god, and many sought to punish those of us who did not follow this dark new religion. Never before have I seen such a time, when man could sink so low. Fear, hate and hysteria reached unimaginable levels—to say nothing of despair. Fathers turned on sons, daughters turned on mothers. The old turned on the sick, the sick turned on the deformed, and the deformed turned on children. All would be taken to the top of the temples and feel the hot sting of the knife.

I am rambling. There is only so much one can repeat words of death and despair and unendurable horror before they lose all meaning and the rampant grotesquery becomes commonplace. I will speak then of the noise that signalled the end—or rather the end of one thing and the coming of another.

It was a noise like a reverse sucking that filled the air, as though the sky was being pulled inside out, and as it carried across the land we gagged and vomited at the stench. I stood atop the Great Temple, and with my final reserve of strength I willed myself to look into Quetzacthulhu's ancient cragged eyes. If there was anything resembling mankind there in those abyssal suns, if he in his immemorial and unknowable existence ever felt even a shade of the things that men did, then I believe I knew what the noise was.

Quetzacthulhu had yawned. He had grown tired.

I am weary myself. I feel like I have lived many lifetimes of men. Here, have the beetle and silence your feeble moaning. I am near the end of my tale anyway.

It was the strangest and saddest thing, what happened. Any relief we should have experienced at the conclusion of such a threat to our existence was washed away in tides of shame and self-pitying sickness. For what did this antediluvian nightmare do but return to the earth from which he had sprouted, and fall into the deepest sleep?

Perhaps he was a god, or an instrument of the gods, here to deliver us divine punishment. Perhaps he came from the underworld and perhaps he came from the earth and perhaps he came from the stars. God or not, we still fought him—we had that right. We threw everything we had at him, and in the end it mattered nought. Most of the time I do not believe we even gained his attention. Unlike the priests—who hailed his sleep as proof that the sacrifices were not in vain, and they had at last appeased his thirst—I do not believe his purpose was one of divine vengeance. Think me blasphemous if you wish, but we were nothing to him. Nothing.

Do you know what is to have the strongest your civilisation can offer ignored, for all your almighty and self-crippling effort, for all the countless deaths to be entirely meaningless? Whereas before it was only our minds that had been warped, now we felt wounded within our very souls, our pride shattered beyond repair. It seemed to some, as the priests cheered and hailed victory, that the gods had denied us; perhaps once we were a cherished golden people, made from divine blood and the bones of the dead, but now we were nought but the dirt under their fingernails.

Those with any strength and sanity left—myself included, women and children included—buried the beast. It took thousands of us, and great movements of earth. It says something of our mental state that we could allow ourselves to get so close to the thing, after all we had seen. And still we heard him—but now the rumble was that of a low, muffled snoring.

We planted seeds in the earth, hoping that if such profane soil had grown plants and trees before it would do so again, and perhaps if the life was good and beautiful enough it might negate the evil, or at least lock the thing within a terrestrial prison. I do not know what we were thinking, but the thoughts were not those of rational men.

Yes, we planted like madmen, and like madmen we also began to build things there, as though the weight of structures could keep the mighty Quetzacthulhu down if ever he decided to wake. I think our actions over the following moons were those of people who had lost all sight of reality, and who were keeping at bay as long as possible the abhorrent and harrowing knowledge of what had been done to us, and of what we had done to ourselves.

I know now—only now, reading these desperate inscriptions. One thousand years, that is what we have. He came before, a thousand years ago, and before that, and before that—way back when Cipactli roamed the endless seas, when jaguars fought giants and sun gods fell and the world was destroyed many times. This was him. He is the lost element to our creation, the thing invisible, the thing between the lines—always there, never read. Until now.

We were a strong people, and the world was stronger than he knew it, but each time he has come he is also stronger. The more lives he can take the greater his next rebirth, his awakening. This time he has quenched himself like never before.

Yes, he will come again, a thousand years hence. He will come, and there is nothing that can stop that. I can feel no relief for our people—we are already defeated. My weakened heart can only bleed for those of the future.

I do not know how long Quetzacthulhu had spent wandering and crushing our land and the lands of our neighbours and once enemies, before he returned to slumber. Time holds no meaning when you are living in a state of perpetual tragedy, when every passing second is a nightmare from which there is no awakening.

All I know is that as the foul presence of Quetzacthulhu dwindled from the land, so too did our people return to some semblance of clarity. With it, fear was replaced by rage. The priests—who were seen as the architects of all that had befallen us, and in some ways they were, certainly they had until now been the only ones bar Moctezuma himself who had escaped harm—were hunted down and butchered. The people stormed over them in a furious tide; I have never before witnessed such cruelty and animal viciousness. I kept my distance from the mobs, though I am certain I glimpsed acts of triumphant cannibalism.

Eventually the energy required to maintain that level of hate burned itself out, and the land returned to silence and peace—though it was far from a happy peace. We walked the leftovers of our once magnificent civilisation in a state of almost catatonic numbness. The scope of what—and who—we had lost in such a short space of time was beyond our ability to comprehend—those that did either committed suicide or lost what remained of their minds; we found mercy in these moments, easing suffering by putting the mad to rest.

There is one last thing to think of. I told you of the coming of something else. You know of what I speak.

I remember the cry taken up, the first strong words heard in many moons—though still wracked with uncertainty and confusion. I was near the sea at the time, and I was one of the first to see, though not one of us understood.

Coming towards us was a vision that made us fall to our knees. There were great castles on the water, and on these stood what seemed to be spirits.

The remaining priests—those who had miraculously kept favour by turning with the tides—together with various chiefs and even Moctezuma himself, fawned over these newcomers when they arrived, and offered them endless treasures. They were greeted as the divine host set to save us from the unimaginable horrors promised us by Quetzacthulhu. There was much rejoicing and wonder, for it was said that our prayers had been answered and our mountains of sacrifice had not been in vain, but there was also not a little fear, for these people were like nothing we had seen before, and all instruments of the gods are to be feared as well as worshipped.

And yet despite the promises made and prophecies fulfilled, doubt seeded in my breast. Beneath me Quetzacthulhu slept, his soft rumbling manifesting itself in the eternal tremble of the earth. I looked at these men—for men they were. I looked at their pale hard faces like ghosts, or the gravebound. I looked at the dull silver they wore on their chests and heads, and clutched in their hands like sticks. I looked at the beasts they pulled off their ships, huge hornless deer, snorting and eyes rolling in their sockets.

And I looked at the way they looked at us, and I wondered.

•　　•　　•

So, there you have it. It is done.

If only I had known then what I know now. Though I ask myself would it have made a difference?

Have you understood any of what I have told you, white man? I hope you know at least a little of my language, for your sake.

You wonder why I have told you this. The world has seen too much blood, even white man's blood. I have told you the story and now I command you to remember and spread the word, for the lives of countless innocents will depend on it—if ever your people have innocence.

A thousand years, you hear me? One thousand years from this date he will wake. Quetzacthulhu will be even stronger after this sleep, I know he will. You may come to call him by another name. But he will wake and he will wreak terrible slaughter and devastation, he will crush your people to nothing, a shadow of a shadow.

You look at me like you do, but you do not know. You never saw what we once were. Every great empire at its peak finds the monstrous within.

I tell you again to remember, to convince all you see and not let your pride overtake you. That is the condition on your freedom white man. You must never forget, you must prepare against it, you must build your whole culture around it!

Do not look at me like that! You must remember, you *must*!

THE HALF SCHOOL

There was only one time in my adult life that I've experienced something that made me doubt reality, and believe that maybe, just maybe, something was being hidden from me.

I was twenty-three, at least I think I was, and I was revisiting my old secondary school. It was the school that had shaped me into a half-formed thing, and it was only after I left that I found the freedom and courage to mould myself into what I am today—not quite fully formed, ever growing inside, but a damn sight better than that hopeless, timid, weasely thing that fell about school like a lump from a vat, a science experiment gone wrong.

It was the school that had nurtured me, a surrogate concrete-and-carpets parent who didn't know a thing about raising a child, treading always the fine line of abuse. It was the school that had scared me, sickened me inside, and crushed me to pulp, and it would hang over me like a great black cloak for the rest of my life.

I would dream of that school forever.

I'd moved eight times since then, three of which involved moving county, searching for something I never found. Which wasn't surprising, as I didn't really know what I was looking for. I hadn't been back to the town my school nested in. There'd been no good reason to.

But the school and those distorted memories of it hung over my head, clouding my progress of *self*, and no matter where I'd go in my life I'd always see those corridors, those faces.

When you dream enough of a real place, and never give it the opportunity to solidify itself by visiting it, then the reality of the place starts to dissolve. It slowly ceases to become real.

This is what happened with the school. I have not re-visited my primary school, but I imagine if I did it would have a similar effect—stronger in some ways, even less real, but weaker in others, less inclined to bad memories and old, ugly wounds of the mind.

A friend and I drove up to the school. He had been there too, in the year below. We hadn't really known each other then, only after.

I mentioned the dreams, but only briefly. I couldn't explain properly, and I didn't want to. There are some things you don't try to explain, at least not out loud.

We walked in, knowing we weren't supposed to be there. I was wearing a leather jacket, my hair purposefully messy. Already things were extremely unusual, to a degree beyond what I could have ever imagined.

I felt like I was walking in one of my own dreams. The fabric of the place was watery; I could run my fingers through the air that floated the corridors and I could *feel* it, I could feel my fingers passing through it like it came in waves of silk, but heavy, and blurry— everything was slightly blurry, just like it was in the dream. Not exactly blurry to the sight, but to the touch, to the senses: the sense of thought, the sense of perception.

I was in a submerged place, an ocean of learning and bullying, something that didn't step to the beat of normal space-time, but flowed on its own lazy currents. I suddenly understood how the guy in *The Truman Show* must have felt, for it seemed that all along I had been in my own Truman Show, my own fake reality, but one constructed of thoughts and spaces. Each place built just for me, at just the right time for my use; except now I had broken the plan, going back to a place I was never supposed to return to.

They had not been expecting my coming, and so had had little time to prepare. As a result, this half-made thing that was the school and its people. Fragile and transient, and almost, *almost* translucent to the touch. It wobbled and it wavered, and the carpeted floors and the white walls never quite matched up. I would not have been too surprised if I could push through the walls, moulding them before me like soft clay. Then I would see what lay beyond.

I didn't push through. I wanted to, in hindsight I should of, but I was carried along like you are in dreams, never really questioning, never really trying to push through.

I remarked several times to my friend how weird it was, how I felt like I was dreaming. The words seemed trite to my ears, in contrast to what was happening. He nodded and seemed to agree, but I knew he wasn't the same, that this place was not acting on him as it did me.

Everything was so small, so strange, and if I had expected to point everything out in quick, delighted recognition, I was disappointed. I recognised nothing absolutely, but I couldn't put my finger on what had changed. Everything seemed to be sinking, half in memory, half in the concoctions of dreams. I could put my hand on a wall and believe it was real, but the same could happen in a dream, and it was the same kind of awareness: being tricked by the mind, walking through water, never really knowing if you were recognising something from memory or something from another dream—or if you truly recognised nothing.

I wandered in a daze in this dollhouse, and as I did various dolls and moving mannequins stared at us, many of them stopping dead. I had expected attention, but not to the degree we got. Perhaps I was wrong in thinking we could have passed ourselves off as sixth-formers. But maybe there was more to it, they reacted with the kind of almost hostile wonder that figments in a dream do when they know you—the dreamer, the controller—are mentally awake and aware, and studying with far too great a gaze that which should remain waterlogged and fuzzy to the unconscious mind.

They could see the doubt ridden across my face, and their eyes followed me.

A clutch of teenage girls said hi to me as I passed. I said hi back, confused. A feeling was creeping up on me, a sensation of dust on me, of a gauzy layer of filth under my skin. I felt dirty, unclean.

I was sure that somebody somewhere, as though whispering it over a long-distance phone-call, was calling me a paedophile. Saying, in a hushed yet quite rabid tone, *'Is this the Mail? Listen . . . there's a strange old man wandering the halls of the school, he looks pretty dodgy to me . . . you know what I mean . . .'*

That is not an encouraging sensation.

I am not an old man.

I'm not even a man.

We decided not to go upstairs to the next level of this place. We were slightly scared, anxious and trying not to show it. We knew we were not allowed to be there, but we hoped that being ex-students we'd have a good enough excuse to be sent out without getting into trouble.

Besides, the geography was all wrong. The way the place was set out, how one point would connect to another. I thought, having spent six years of my life with that school, that I would be on very familiar home turf. Instead I felt like an intruder, a parasite, leeching off the dull, warbling energy this made-up building and its grounds possessed. I didn't know where I was, or what I was doing. My body seemed to remember, by instinct and muscle memory (*left* two three four, *right* two three four), and it led the way, and with each step my mind boggled and marvelled, at how something could be real and yet not.

We walked the outside of the school, by the playing field, and a tall boy stared at me harder than any other. I caught his gaze immediately, and I stared him down. He had an astounded, verging on aggressive *what the fuck* expression on his face, and I wonder to this day if his mouths actually formed the words. What was the problem, hadn't he seen someone like me before? Did I have a horse's face, did I have a tail and udders?

I continued to stare him down until we rounded a corner. I'd won. It was a microscopic victory by itself, not worth mentioning for most people, but to me it meant something, and I would always remember it. I'd never stood up to people at school. I guess what I'd really wanted in coming back here, was not to relish nostalgia, but to *fight*, fight my past, share minds with the child with my name who used to come here and to fight his wrongdoers and oppressors, fight and slay everybody who ever made him feel weak and small.

I couldn't go back in time. But this place—I'm not sure time was even working here. When I checked my phone after we left, we'd only been there for minutes.

More girls looked at me.

I remembered when a friend at school—one of those friends who you're never really sure if they even *are* your friend—once said I looked like a troll. I thought of those huge, misshapen things that lived under bridges. I wasn't huge. And I didn't live under a bridge. I never had.

I can't remember if we were beckoned to the front desk, or we approached it ourselves. Either way we were done. We didn't mind leaving. I was worried that something terrible would happen if I stayed; or something not terrible, but amazing and utterly uncertain, and that can be even scarier.

My friend chatted with the front desk receptionist while three teenage girls behind me giggled.

'My friend thinks you're attractive,' one of them called out, or at least I think they did. I genuinely do not know if this happened or not. I do not know if any of this happened.

'Thanks,' I said, trying to be cool but feeling anything but. I didn't ask which friend. They were too young by some margin.

'How do you get your hair like that?' the girl said again.

'Um. Backcombed.' I felt that slightly dirty feeling again, but staying in the front of the school and communicating with these people made me feel a bit more in control. The world was solidifying in this spot, relieved that they could structure and harden things around me.

There was the uncomfortable, greasy feeling, the self-convincing *I'm not a pervert I'm just accepting a compliment*, but I also couldn't help but smile to myself, and feel bigger, brasher, confident and attractive.

I remember when a girl at school asked me out as a joke.

Balancing confidence and social discomfort is a hard act, and thankfully no more questions were asked, and I did not submit any of my own.

As we left, returning to my friend's car, I felt such a myriad of emotions that I could not help but keep them at bay, lest they swarm and bamboozle me completely. How can one suffer such tangling, contradicting emotions as joy and loss, self-confidence and anger, guilt and empowerment, bewilderment and satisfaction? How does one wake from sleepwalking? I kept my head down, and talked idle nothings to my friend.

We left that dollhouse, that half school, and it hardened behind us.

Thinking back on it now, I can't tell you what did happen, and what did not happen. I am remembering it like a dream of a dream. I have never known a place as it exists in the sleeping mind to exact itself so similarly in reality.

All I know is that there exists at least three people. There is the child who went to that school, who studied and didn't study, who fidgeted and doodled and shivered with nerves, and was punched casually in the head at least once a day. That child is not me. He was never me. I simply replaced him.

There is me. I do not know what I am. Not yet. I only know what I am not.

Then there is a third person, who to that day I did not know existed. This is the half-person who was there on that singular visit to that malleable half-school. He was a sleepwalker, a vision quester, neither child nor adult, neither past nor present, but stuck in between, tied to all, and seeing the future.

I haven't been back to that school. But if I want to find that person again, then I know just where to go.

I would dream of that dream of a school forever.

THE GAUNTLET OF GORE

I n the middle of the green glowing field there was a stage, old and wooden, such that a theatre troupe might perform on. On this stage were sat the principal players of Stonewaters Bookstore, all dressed in green, green gowns and green tunics and the like, with their long hair braided or tied back in tails. Sitting about the field facing the stage were many more of these players, and among them assorted small groups of the opposing teams: St Aidens, Trinity, and William Howard School. Everybody looked to the stage in interest. Nobody had played Stonewaters before; after all, they were a bookstore, not a school. Some of them wondered what the hell the Organisers were thinking.

Sarah and Mike were late, and the closer they walked to the crowd, the more the tension became apparent. A girl in elegant braids was speaking from her chair on the stage. Her words reached them, and they knew she was deeply afraid.

'What's going on?' Mike said, under his breath.

'Look at everyone,' Sarah replied. 'There's more noise at a graveyard. Look at their faces.'

Mike scanned the groups, and saw how even those of the teams opposing Stonewaters had fixed, mute expressions, poker faces every one.

'. . . pleased as much as we are with our new captains,' the girl on stage continued, her voice tremulous, her eyes pleading, 'and hope they will see Stonewaters to an easy and triumphant victory!'

A hard applause greeted the words, which died as abruptly as it began.

'Hypnotised?' whispered Mike, moving through the groups to an empty patch of grass.

'Nuh . . . o,' said Sarah, hesitantly. 'I don't think so.' She caught the eye of a fellow William Howard player, and his eyes did the talking for them. *They're terrified*, she thought.

She waved a hand in the air at the stage. 'Oi, woodelves!' she shouted, at Mike sat fast on the floor and tried to pull her down next to him. 'Any chance you could bring your fucking captains back out for the latecomers?'

The braided girl's eyes widened, and then she turned her head to the side, listening, her whole body visibly trembling as shadows moved behind her.

The girl cleared her throat. 'The captains are more than happy to make another appearance.' She shrank then, becoming diminutive and unimportant, and a chill swept through the crowd, though no faces changed to show it.

'What did you have to go and do that for,' said Mike unhappily. 'I've got goosebumps.'

'Looks like you're not the only one,' Sarah replied. 'Look how stiff everyone is. Like shop dummies.'

They came out then, three of them, and Sarah would have burst out laughing if not for their faces, if not for the cold, scared applause of the hundreds of bodies around her, the undercurrent of dread rippling its way unseen through the crowd and touching her on the shoulders.

They were dressed as mascots, absurd, dumb mascots. One was a loaf of bread. One was a bottle of milk. One was a bag of sugar. They would have been laughable, senseless camp counsellors or perhaps auditioning for some TV food advert.

But for their faces.

Their smiles were too big to fit, too big for their skin, which stretched and contorted around the edges of their face. They were ghastly visages meant more for a nightmare circus than a sports crowd. Their thick, rubbery lips went up to their ears, as though pulled by hooks, around skin the quality of waxy dough, or half-melted plastic. Above those garish grins turned unblinking eyes, round and bulging like two stuck marbles.

'Greetings again everyone,' said the woman captain, the bottle of milk flanked by two men. 'It seems we're due for a second speech.' She spoke through her smile, with a high, scabrous tone, like a rat trying to talk. The teeth were short and sickly white, draped over by the excess of fat pink gums. Sarah wasn't right up to the stage, but she could see enough, and as the woman's mouth moved she detected an almost hidden sharpness inside, a row of points just emerging from the gums, trying to wriggle out.

'Please sit down, my foul-mouthed dearie,' said the woman captain, and Sarah sat down. The woman raised her hands, old hands belonging more to a crone than what Sarah would have guessed was somebody middle-aged, and she began her speech.

Sarah and Mike listened, transfixed by those awful smiles, those brief glints of points in the mouth, those long, wrinkled fingers gesturing, but when the woman clapped her hands and gave a short, stilted bow, they realised they had remembered nothing. All they could think of was a kind of droning noise, a low, flat hum that had only just ended, their ears suddenly unblocked and the world silent and clear.

The two men on either side of the woman, the bread and the sugar mascots, gave their own stiff bows, and the silence was crashed by a quick, razor-sharp beating of hands. Even Sarah found herself smacking her hands together so hard they hurt, and looking to her side she saw Mike doing the same, his face confused and terribly scared.

The captains left the stage, and palpable relief shuddered through the crowd. The braided girl came out, her face quivering, trying to hold herself composed but her words coming out rushed and stuttering. People started to trail away from the stage, and Sarah got up, pulling a dazed Mike with her, and the two of them walked away.

'What happened . . . who *were* they... those *smiles* . . . I can't remember a thing she said,' Mike was saying, and Sarah was nodding, feeling distant and drifting.

'What does this mean for the game?' Mike pressed her, and touched her arm when she didn't respond.

She jerked a little, then her shoulders slumped. 'It means that it's going to get interesting,' she said. 'C'mon, maybe our captain has some idea. Some of the others must have seen the earlier announcements.'

The William Howard lodge came up over the crest of a hill, and they instantly felt clearer of head when they passed under the school's heraldry. They strode with renewed vigour through the pine arches and into the main cabin, which was roaring with noise and sweating with the heat of a dozen bodies.

Everybody was talking and arguing and shouting at once, and from what Sarah could gather, most of it was about the other teams, chiefly Stonewaters Bookstore.

'*Those smiles* -'

'- A dwarf *and* a giant -'

'- some kind of black magic, I know it -'

'- all new players, don't know what -'

'- just a trick, don't worry, just a strategy to mess with us -'

'- *and* a giant as siege -'

A loud fizzing sound ending in a *snap* shut everyone's attempts at being heard dead. The huge plasma screen that occupied one wall of the cabin had caught life. It was divided by borders into three, but it was the same picture, and it was that of bare whiteness containing a single figure: a man in the middle section, raising his hands and calling for attention, though it was not needed.

'Now listen, guys,' the man on the TV started, dropping his hands. 'I know everybody has concerns. A new team, yes a *bookstore* at that, and some scary looking captains to boot. And yes, Dave, I do know of those siege weapons, and yes they are a dwarf and a . . . exceptionally tall player. He's new to this, and should be an easy take if we've got the right tactics, but the dwarf comes from another team, I don't know which, another country I think, and he's a dab hand. But look at me. Look at me. Do you think this bothers me? Do you think this should bother any of you?' The man pointed at his calm face, his eyes hidden by sunglasses, and when some of the team players started murmuring and somebody seemed on the verge of addressing the problem rather more loudly the man raised up his hands again.

'Listen. Everyone. We are William Howard School. We have won the game the last three times. This is an *experienced* team. In fact, we only have three new players, since last year's *triumph.*' - At this some of the more confident players gave a *whoop.* - 'And not only that, he continued, 'but an entire *half* the team have played for three years. That, my friends, is *unprecedented.*' More whoops, and more smiles returning. Sarah felt encouraged, but she also felt a little sick. She didn't feel like seeing anybody smile for some time.

Their captain walked across the screen, and the man who appeared on the separated right section of television was older, wiser, with grey hair and a grey suit. It was still the same man. His sunglasses were now glasses, and he peered at them with pale blue eyes.

'You want,' he began, with weathered certainty, 'a strategy. I will give you it. Sit down. This will take some time, and it will be late by the time I have finished, and then we will continue tomorrow morning. I trust you are already fit, and trained, as best you can with those dummy gauntlets. For those three of you new to this game'—he looked pointedly at a trio of boys, only one of whom looked at all confident, and one of whom looked like he was going to piss his pants—'tomorrow afternoon will make or break. The shower of gore has sent some players away screaming, or curled into a ball, senses lost, just as it has turned boys to men and girls to women, and both boys and girls into players of the Gauntlet. You will not know what you can take until you are in the field, but I hope, particularly in this age of extreme bloody violence on every channel you can turn to, every videogame you can play, every film, song, painting, book, that you will not mind getting a little red on you.' Cue laughter from the experienced players, bar Sarah.

So they sat and listened to the talk. It went on for hours, as their captain told them each of their roles, and what he'd learned about the other teams, bolstering bad rumours, how Trinity was training only in virtual reality, at least half the team hooked on pleasure enhancers—*nerds*, the team jeered, laughing at how soft and weak they would be. He told them about their own siege weapon—a quiet boy at the back of the room, called Freddy, and how, while he was new to this, he was going to be devastating to the opposing teams. He talked about their tactics for the dwarf and giant, the only names they were referred to by now. They were the siege players for St Aiden's and Trinity respectively—everybody got one siege, the term given to a unusual player who was chosen to pose a challenge to other teams, a figure perhaps difficult to destroy, or difficult to defend against. They'd faced a dwarf before, three years ago. They were siege because the punch in the stomach required to unleash the power of the gauntlet was harder to aim for, given the difference in height. It was the same with the giant, although they'd never faced a particularly tall player before. His height was unknown, as neither the captain nor his sources had seen him, presumably because Trinity were playing their cards close to their chest, as usual.

The captain talked as outside the sun waned and drooped, fielding questions from the players, describing on-field tactics, the wider strategy, a run-through of defence and offense moves, both classic and new. 'The more new moves we can adapt to,' the captain said, 'the more of an edge we'll have. We need to know how to defend ourselves against these moves, and how to surprise the opposition with moves they've never prepared for. They are absolutely crucial.'

They'd trained for all of these, already, for weeks beforehand, but that didn't matter. Everything had to be perfect when one's life was at stake, a fact the captain had to drum into one of the new boys when he saw through the videolink that the boy was drifting off, nearly asleep. 'Look at the others!' he thundered. 'Awake, and so sharp you could whet knives on them! Why do you think that is? Because they don't want to die, and they don't want their friends to die!'

The first part was certainly true, although playing the Gauntlet was always a tremendous gamble, well-practiced or not. As for the second, most of the experienced players (being anybody who had survived more than one game) knew better than to make friends. Sarah had Mike, but she had conditioned herself to accept his death, if it came. You quickly learned how to adapt to losing people around you. It wasn't really loss, anymore, merely the facts of the game. Rather like a war, except you fought in a war because you were told to, and often even the victorious weren't seen as heroes. The Gauntlet you played because you wanted to, because you were good at it, or thought you'd be, and if you won you were a hero, an icon, a *fucking rockstar*.

Their televised captain hammered on at them, switching between his middle self, his old self, and his young self, who swaggered about the left hand side with long hair and an open t-shirt, chuckling and cracking jokes, raising cheers. They weren't the only one with an A.I. captain; apparently Trinity had one too now, although nobody had ever seen him, or her. St Aiden's captain was a strict, tight-lipped woman always in some kind of blazer, and it was rumoured that she drilled the team mercilessly.

Eventually, their captain summed up, raised his arms, and prompted an ovation, running between the borders of the TV, changing age and appearance without even a flicker. He stopped in the middle, out of breath, thanked them, announced a 6:00am start tomorrow (to which nobody groaned), and the TV shot to darkness.

Sarah took to the showers with Mike and the others, some staying behind to practise moves, or read books on the game. Some went to bed right away, and some sat up rocking and whispering to themselves.

She let the hard water run over her, slashing at the dead skin and dirt, at the tiredness of her body after her journey here. From another stall she heard sounds of pleasure—two in a stall, she thought—and then cries of shock and laughter as others discovered them and ripped the curtain back. And then another cry, louder and more piercing, rising above the pound of the water, and as she looked up, as though she might see the culprit voice embodied on the ceiling, she saw the hot breath of the showers rolling and folding into a cloud of red steam.

There was the *shill* sound of a curtain yanked, and a race of footsteps. She pulled her curtain around her face to see a boy, the same nervous, piss-his-pants new boy, run gasping and bleating, as red and dripping as an oversized abortion.

Two other boys were following him at a trot, laughing, and catching up to him when the boy slipped and hit the floor, pooling in blood. He lay there like the carcass of a pig, his eyes glassy and staring, his dick drowned and dead like some tiny sacrificial totem.

'You turn it the other way mate,' chuckled one of the boys, as others leaned out from their shower stalls to jeer.

Sarah left her stall and strode over the boy, as around her the other players gasped and giggled at her naked form. She pulled the bloodied boy up by the hand and led him to an empty shower, which she turned on, *the right way*, and soon the drain was sucking away all that red horror.

She stayed in the shower, helping the shivering boy wash, as outside came the inevitable chants of *Sarah's got a boyfriend, Sarah's got a boyfriend!*

'What . . . why . . .' started the boy, as she took his hands and poured shampoo in them, guiding them up to his hair and into the motions, until he carried on doing it mechanically by himself.

'Why did the shower rain blood?' she prompted.

He nodded, and his eyes found their life again, and looked into hers.

She shrugged. 'Sometimes it's a way for some players to celebrate a victory. Sometimes it's a pre-match thing, like a war-chant or something. Sometimes it's like an initiation, for new players. I never do it, myself.' *But you did,* said a voice inside her. *You used to.*

'What . . . whose blood is it? Is it human?'

'I don't know. I never thought to ask.' *Yes you did. You just didn't want the answer.*

The boy said nothing more, but he seemed to be recovering from the shock—the shock of not just opening his eyes to see the shower was spurting a fountain of warm, sticky blood all over him, but also the falling over, the lying curled on the floor, naked among people he barely knew, stunned and wounded by their laughter.

'My name's Joseph,' he said quietly.

'Okay. I'm Sarah. I'm leaving you to it now Joseph, alright?'

Sarah left the stall, and heard his mumbled thank you behind her. As she strode off purposefully through the shower room, back to her stall, she glared at the heads of the boys and girls who looked round their curtains as she passed. The two older boys who had followed the new kid, laughing as he ran and tripped, were stood about, cocky despite their nakedness. She knew them from last year's team: Daniel and Jack.

They were following her as they had followed Joseph, but without running, without laughing. She felt their smirks as they watched her behind like the lion watches the gazelle. *Except this gazelle is in disguise. This gazelle is a bigger lion.*

One of them, perhaps dared through meaningful eye-contact by the other, plucked up the nerve to smack her ass. She span around, and saw Jack's arm dart back, his eyes alight, grinning with puerile delight at how her soft flesh had felt to his touch. Daniel was laughing. Then their gazes dropped to her breasts, and lower down too.

Sarah reached forward and grabbed Jack's arm, the same arm that had smacked her, and she pulled it towards her. 'Come on then,' she said brusquely. 'Have a shower with me.'

'What?' His smirk was still there, but it looked different, touched with confusion, with a hint of fear. It was a for-show smirk now, there for appearances in the face of Daniel and the others.

'I said come on. You want me, well come get me.' She yanked him harder, and, as she predicted, he resisted. *The harder you pull, the harder they pull back.*

'You some kinda slut?' interjected Daniel.

'Yes, that's exactly what I am,' said Sarah, her steely eyes turning to him. 'I'm a slut. The biggest kind of slut. I want you too Daniel. Both of you, at the same time. Come on.'

Now the both of them looked unsure of themselves, all pretence at smirking gone. Around them, heads were whispering and murmuring, or staring in silence. Out of the corner of her eye she saw Mike's head, and she knew he was grinning.

'Fuck off,' Jack said, pulling away again at her, but her grip was iron tight. The hold of his feet stuttered, and he was dragged two steps against his will. 'Hey, get off!' he exclaimed, looking angry and frightened.

'Let go of him!' said Daniel.

She looked pointedly down at them, at Jack and Daniel's penises, and as they realised where she was looking, the two of them went red. 'Oh,' she said softly, but loud enough for everyone to hear. 'You're virgins, is that it? Well, I can't say I'm surprised. I can't see you being able to do much with *those* things.' She put her other hand up to her mouth to *not quite* suppress a giggle.

At last, she let Jack tear his arm away from her, and he rubbed it aggressively, as though she had actually hurt him. The two of them backed off, sullen, embarrassed and beaten.

'Bitch,' said Daniel, his parting shot as they went to get their clothes.

'You better believe it,' she said, and walked back to her shower, as always, unconcerned with covering herself. *Shame is the first step to being a victim,* she thought to herself. *The hidden fruit is twice as sweet. You can't make me go red, I own this body, and you can go fuck yourselves.*

Anyway, tomorrow, chances are you'll be dead.

•   •   •

The next morning, the sun rose with a reddish glare, as though it knew of the blood sport to come, and was eager to be the first spectator. The sky was cloudless, and the day built up hot and harsh. Outside the stalks of grass shimmered, stretching out, anxiously awaiting the nutrients that were to spatter down on them.

When playing the Gauntlet, there are two options. Either you win, or the whole team dies.

Either you die, or you see every other opposing team member blown to bits. There are no corpses, only giblets.

The odds were stacked against every player. There was a very high chance this was the day they would die. Reckless courage and the arrogance of ego were the measures by which they fought this statistical probability. Team spirit and unity were the banners they waved against the spectre of death.

This morning, for the first time in years, there was something else on the players' minds.

It started out as a rumour, and was dismissed by the captains and the experienced players as such. It was said, circulating among the teams, that Stonewaters Bookstore were losing players, and replacing them just as fast.

'Don't be ridiculous,' Mike had said. 'The game hasn't even started yet, how could they be losing players?'

Then two players from St Aidens School saw the ropes hung from the Stonewaters lodge, twisted in nooses and glistening, and as they came closer they saw that they were not ropes but intestines. They were hooked and looped over nails hammered in to the roof. On the end of each intestine were the nooses, cut and tied to themselves. The other ends were hidden, trailing out and up from the open stomachs of the dead.

Flies buzzed around the bodies of the Stonewaters players, though they had not been up long, and summer crows croaked overhead, waiting to land. The players were wearing their team garb, and they had been strangled by their own guts.

Soon half the players of every team had seen them for their own eyes.

'I don't get it,' said Alex, a loud-voiced girl from last year. 'Why would the Stonewaters captains kill their own players? If they're going to kill someone before the game starts, why not those of the other teams?'

'Because that'd be breaking the rules,' replied Sarah. 'You can't interfere with the players of other teams before a match or you forfeit the game, and sometimes worse. There's nothing in the rules about killing your own.'

'But why do it? Why sabotage your own team?'

'Fear, I guess. Maybe they're not sabotaging the team. Maybe they're cutting out the weak. I bet they have a horde of reserves, and they're building their very first team the best it can be. All strong potential players, all fierce, unquestioning, players who don't fear death so much as they fear their captains.'

Alex and the others gaped at her, while the William Howard captain listened silently. 'But . . . but what does that mean?' Alex said at last.

'It means,' Sarah said, 'that they might be hard to beat.'

•   •   •

They trained hard throughout the morning, prepared both physically and mentally by the three incarnations of their captain.

Outside, a wireless screen was wheeled out for the young captain to lead them through their exercises and plays with the dummy gauntlets; occasionally the screen changed its channel so the man in the sunglasses could offer advice and tactics.

By the end of their training, reports of three more deaths had come to them, three more Stonewaters players hung up by their intestines by their monstrous captains.

If the lodge had been loud yesterday, today it was full of whispers. Perhaps, seemed to be the unspoken idea, if everybody talked under their breath, then the evil that touched the Stonewaters Bookstore couldn't hear them, couldn't affect them.

One of the few not talking in whispers was Sarah, and she was frustrated with the cobwebbed words of the others, the furtive glances, the hunched postures. She knew they were encouraging fear, inviting it in, by acting this way. They were making it *real*.

The captain appeared on screen. This was the older man, searching them out with a put-on look of both care and challenge. Even the A.I. understood the seriousness of the situation. More intelligent than any of them, he was extremely adaptable and self-learning. *But a day as absurd and horrific as this must have stretched him*, Sarah thought. She'd have doubted him, as she once did, but that was before he had led them to victory for three years in a row, with minimal casualties.

'Okay, everybody,' he said. 'I'm going to give you a last talk, and I want you all to listen. Afterwards, I'll take questions. I know about what's bothering you, but it can wait. Strategy is more important right now than answering the call of fear. I ask you all to keep your heads.'

He spent half an hour going over everything again in brief, focusing on the important buzzwords, like that of *co-operation* and *steadfastness*, while the players fidgeted.

Eventually, he sighed, and said after a pause, 'Questions.'

Just about every hand in the room shot up.

The captain blinked. 'Yes,' he said, pointing at someone in the front row, a girl named Juliet.

'What the fuck is with the Stonewaters captains? They're *monsters!*'

The hands in the room went slowly down.

The captain said nothing for a few seconds. 'Yes,' he said at last. 'I have not encountered such opposing forces before. But their methods are not beyond me, and it is imperative you understand them. They wish to make their team afraid, so that they are loyal, and aggressive. Anything to get away from their captains, I'm sure. They wish to make *you* afraid, afraid and bewildered, so that you will not want to fight the Stonewaters players, so that every glimpse you have of their captains will make you shudder and forget yourself, and so, of course, that you will be with your fear at crucial moments, and not with your head in the game. Fear from behind us bolsters us, drives us, while fear from in front makes us grind to a halt, or turn our tails and run.

'I will not use fear in my tactics with you. Nor, despite what is said about the St Aidens and Trinity captains, do they. I believe in a common strength, and in bravery, not in quaking players looking behind as much as in front. Their players are driven senseless by the executions of their friends. You should have little doubt that their final team will be quite mad, and quite reckless. You should know, then, that this is their greatest weakness, and it is what has shaped my training of you over the second half of the morning.'

He shot out a finger. 'Tell me, Sarah, who won, the Roman phalanxes or the barbarian hordes?'

Sarah figured he wasn't asking for a history lesson, and promptly replied, 'The Romans.'

'Correct,' he said. 'As we will beat Stonewaters Bookstore today. Let their fear be their downfall. Let their frantic aggression trip them up. Let their wild swings be uncontrolled and clumsy, and easily dodged. Let them come at you with their bull-headed charges, and be their matador.

'Of course,' he added, 'don't forget about the other teams. Yes, you.' He nodded at a boy called Paul, who had his hand back up in the air.

'What was with their outfits during the announcement? I mean, bread, milk, sugar was it? It doesn't make any sense!'

The screen flickered for a second, as their captain furrowed his brows. 'Exactly, Paul. Fear and confusion are good bedfellows. One often begets the other. There is, as far as I can tell, neither rhyme nor reason to it. It is merely a distraction, an absurdist play that serves as one more thing to keep your minds not on the game, but on silly riddles with no answer. I tell you all now, forget it! Forget their captains entirely!'

Paul put his hand up again, and the captain nodded curtly at him.

'Who . . . what is Stonewater's siege weapon?' His question was accompanied by murmurs around him, and alert, expectant looks at the captain.

The old man shook his head. 'I am afraid I do not know. They have kept it hidden. I have asked the other team captains, and nobody knows. Whoever the siege is, expect the worst.'

The players grumbled and groaned, and some of the less experienced players were wringing their hands. The new boy Joseph had gone pale, but then he'd been looking ill since the first rumours of Stonewater deaths had passed their way.

•   •   •

The grass were iron blades burnished under the heat of the midday sun. Millions upon millions of little knives, all thirsting, ready to whet their whistles on the redness of humans.

The grounds for play covered the field, the central mud banks where lives were often lost, and the sparse yet dark forests around the fringes, where each team would begin. That's where they waited, so tense you could cut yourself on their muscles. Some shivering, some breathing deep, some with eyes closed and praying to the gods of slaughter.

In no time at all, each of them would look a horror, team colours almost indistinguishable under slopping coats of mud and blood. Fighting, frenzied and frothing, lost in the berserker hazes of battle lust and battle terror. The tactics drilled into them could never last forever, could never be present when you were staring into the rolling whites of enemy eyes. Then, it was just you and them, and your death hung on a seesaw.

The woods were thin, but most of the trunks were wide. In the later stages of the game, sometimes called the hunt, sometimes called clean-up, they would hide players, players shivering and scared, putting off the inevitable, and players silent in their concealment, waiting to assassinate their hunters. Overhead the canopy was thick and heavy from these trees, filling in the gaps and shutting out the sun. The experienced players stood and crouched like panthers in the darkness, feeling the dirt under them and stroking the bark of the trees with their free hand.

You couldn't see the cameras unless you were looking for them, but they were there. They had their places. In the field the cameras were long-range, pointing in at the action from the sidelines, but here they sneaked in among the trees, flicking on and off with night vision to the rapt, hungry attention of their audience.

The spectators sat in their stands on the only side of the field not bordered by woods, munching their processed meats and gurgling beer, keeping eyes on the huge screens that showed the choice views from the cameras, field and forest. The audience who watched at home slunk lower in their fat armchairs, or indulged drunken bloodlusts perched on barstools with their chattering, gasping brethren.

No spectators would cross the boundaries and come onto the pitch. There would be no streakers, no attention-seekers. If you passed the boundaries, your life was forfeit. Neither the Organisers or any player were held responsible if you were hurt, or if you died.

The audience stayed put.

This wasn't as polished a set-up as the Nationals, or the World Titles, but a lot of people preferred the Locals, the inter-school matches. They were amateurs, technically, but the orgy of violence suited them, suited the dirt and roughness of the grounds. There were only a handful of pro stadiums—called Coliseums these days—out there. The players didn't play on fields and in forests and sliding up and down mud banks, but on laminate flooring. Obstacles were varied, with new ones introduced in each game, keeping a novelty element for the audience and a surprise element for the teams. Regular obstacles included a simulated forest made of branchless, leafless poles to dodge, a waxen floor to slip and slide on, and a crowd favourite, an area of connected trampolines. You hadn't seen anything until you'd seen two players jumping towards each other, fists connecting in each other's stomachs, and exploding in mid-air.

Sarah checked her gauntlet for what seemed to be the twentieth time. There was no such thing as over-checking, not when your life depended on it working and staying strapped tight around your hand. She opened the small protective casing, flicked the switch and felt the familiar *thrum*, the vibrations coursing through her fingers and up her arm. When it hit the spot, a stomach, the vibrations, tuned to the perfect frequency, would multiply over and over, rumbling their way through the gauntlet and rippling the enemy's (you better hope they were an enemy) stomach. And then they exploded.

She moved to switch it back off, when a siren sounded, sharp and angry, emitting from every camera. Now she could see them, blinking black and sullen in the trees.

'Switch 'em on!' she shouted, and those players that needed telling did so.

She looked over at Mike, who nodded at her, his face hard. She turned to see Joseph, who had his eyes closed and was muttering fast to himself. She was relieved to see his gauntlet was on and working.

A couple of steps before her, Freddy was stretching. *You better be good*, she thought.

A second noise, higher than the last, and ending faster.

'Everybody!' Sarah shouted. 'You're here now! If you want to turn back, it's too late, you'll just have to fight your way out! Remember your training! Remember your teammates! Fight for your team, fight for your life, fight for William Howard! *Give 'em Hell!*'

A cheer, desperate and aggressive, was echoed by some, and was quickly swallowed by the darkness. Some of them were gulping repeatedly and some were shaking their heads, as though wishing the dream away.

The third call.

They ran.

•　　•　　•

They cleared the forest in whooping, shrieking leaps, and the sun turned its eye right on them, the biggest camera of all.

From the corner of her right eye Sarah saw the blur of a roaring crowd. And from the treeline that fringed the field on all other sides came the enemy.

St Aidens from the left, colour of blue, Trinity from ahead, colour of yellow. Rushing towards them, towards each other, howling like barbarians or wolves, their gauntlets glinting silver in the sun.

Soon we'll all be the same colour, she thought as she ran with the purple-clad William Howard team. *Then it'll be faces that matter. Look them in the eyes, and if you didn't see them in the lodge this morning, kill them.*

There were less St Aidens and Trinity players than William Howard. She knew they would have split their teams, sending some players off through the forest to strike on two (or three) fronts. The William Howard captain had decided to keep their team together, as he had last year. It meant their rear was unprotected, but it also meant they were a unified force, a ram to drive through and overwhelm.

St Aidens players would likely be racing through the forest to take them from behind while they were up to their necks with the others. But the second line of William Howard players were ready to turn at a moment's notice, ready to obstruct their stomachs with the gauntlet and provide an unbreakable rearguard.

That was the theory, at least.

The half-metal gauntlet was the best defence you had against another gauntlet. A blow at full force could break your wrist, if you blocked with your other arm. But the gauntlet was also by far the easiest way to kill your opponent, and so every split second there was a question of defence or offense, to parry or strike. The wrong choice and you would not make another choice ever again.

It was against the game rules to wear padding—to wear anything that touched or came close to the stomach—under your team kit. Their captain had frisked them all before they had moved to their positions. If a player was found to be cheating, apart from capital punishment for the individual, the entire team might never play again.

She could make out the individual faces of the other teams, before she realised what was missing.

Stonewaters Bookstore.

She was so used to playing against only two teams, that she hadn't noticed at first. But the gap between St Aidens and Trinity, now it was obvious. That was where the green-clad players should have sprung from, but they hadn't.

They're all in the forest.

The realisation would come to the other players, if it hadn't already. The Stonewaters would be mounting a defence in the dark, ready to intercept the St Aidens and Trinity players from both sides. Or perhaps they were spreading themselves through the woods, hiding behind trees, *maybe even climbing them*, ready to ambush, guerrilla style. *Sneaky bastards.*

Subterfuge tactics didn't suit William Howard School, and they'd rarely employed them. Head on, hard and powerful, that was them—and for three years it hadn't let them down.

Freddy was ahead of them now. At first just by a couple of paces, and then, as Sarah observed with mounting alarm, at a distance growing every second. 'Slow down Freddy!' she yelled, or tried to—she was panting with exertion, and if Freddy heard her, he didn't look around.

The St Aidens team had divided: one half towards Trinity, one half towards the William Howard team. Trinity, in contrast, were moving their whole team towards the St Aidens players. *You idiots!* thought Sarah at the St Aidens players, and at their captain, who would be watching from between the two barriers that separated the spectators from the players. St Aidens—all but those in the forest—would be wiped out, if by numbers more than anything else. That was good—but massacres weren't. Ideally, St Aidens and Trinity—and Stonewaters, whoever encountered them first—would be evenly matched—allowing for a bloodbath on both sides. Devouring small, shellshocked and exhausted groups was easy—fighting a powerful force pumped up from storming the opposition with minimal losses was not.

On the bright side, with Trinity ignoring them, for now, they could load all guns to bear, so to speak, at the pinch of St Aidens players charging suicidally at them.

Freddy got there first, and his gauntlet arm was thrust out at his side ready for the killing blow.

In a few seconds, Sarah would wish she had access to the slow-motion replays that would have entertained the audience. As it was, it happened too quick and seamless for her to really understand.

A drop of a St Aidens player, to his knees. The dwarf, unstrapping himself from the player's back, vaulting, *leapfrogging*, and then—and then a sunset shower. And the biggest parts of Freddy remaining you could fit in the palm of your hand.

A chunk of flesh slid down the dwarf's grinning face—*that* was the slow-motion bit, that grin, the smear left by the slipping chunk of Freddy.

'*Siege down!*' somebody yelled, and Sarah saw players beside her stumble in their advance, hand up to their face in shock.

'Keep going!' Sarah shouted back. 'No holding back!' She put more encouragement in her voice than she could give to herself. *Freddy the boy wonder, gone minutes into the game, gone before a single kill. Nobody would ever know how good he really was. You were either good, or you were nothing, and Freddy was most certainly nothing now.*

'First blood!' bayed the dwarf, and the two sides met.

Sarah's first move was a spin. A player in blue, his gauntlet ready to thrust, hesitated when confronted with a stomach turned to back, and that hesitation was all Sarah needed. She didn't allow a second for the player to move his gauntlet to one of defence. She felt the THRUM and violent shuddering as her gauntlet connected at the tail end of her spin. The player's mouth opened slackly, gibbering for a mere snapshot of time, before the gauntlet's undulations reduced him to an outwardly expanding spray. Sarah's left arm was up in preparation, shielding her eyes from the rain (one of the most basic and most important tactics to learn, if you didn't want to be half-blinded), and then she was on to the next.

All about, cascades of gore. The sky seemed hell-bent on a scatter-shot deluge of giblets. Her shoulder came into contact with a fellow William Howard player; she felt his whole body convulse, and then he was empty space. She stumbled, and it saved her life; a gauntleted fist came powering through in the spot where she had been, just about stomach height.

She fell to her knees and punched upwards and slanting, ducking her head as her overbalanced attacker oscillated and exploded. Fleshy lumps pattered onto her, and she shook them from her hair. She stood up to see all but two St Aidens players left - a lanky girl with red hair and the dwarf. The girl was guarding her stomach with her gauntlet while punching heads with a left hook, dazing her targets before the gauntlet strike. The dwarf was a small red totem, hammering from below, swift, unpredictable, and hard to hit. Sarah saw him punch Daniel's groin, smacking him in the face when he doubled over, so the boy snapped backwards as quick as he had come. The dwarf jumped in and laid the killing blow, and just like that the boy who had called her a bitch in the showers was gone.

Mike went for the girl, guarding his head with one hand, the elbow in the way of a clean hit to the stomach. He jabbed at her chest and shoulders with his gauntlet, quicker than she could block. He dropped his free hand a little, and her fist instantly shot out for his head. He caught it, and headbutted her in the face. You couldn't tell her nose was broken, not with all that blood, but that little *crunch* had to come from somewhere.

The girl staggered, reeling, and another player came up behind and laid a kick at her spine. She twisted backwards, her gauntlet hand dropped, and as soon as her midriff was exposed Mike turned her into lawn feed.

The other players were crowded around the dwarf, who was dodging and rolling from their attacks, swearing at them and wiping away the blood that dribbled down from his forehead. Sarah looked across the field, ignoring the distant rise and ebb of the crowd as they licked their teeth at the carnage. She checked their backs—no St Aidens players had flanked them. She looked ahead, and saw two St Aidens players running for the woods, survivors of the clash with Trinity. *Fleeing in terror, or luring them to the woods as bait?* she wondered. *Was that the plan all along? I wonder if the boys and girls who were sacrificed to the melee knew the role they were to play.*

Except, as she mopped her brow with her sleeve (she'd never show clean skin, not when the sleeve itself was filthy, but she could at least stop it coming into her eyes) and scanned the crest and rise of the field, the Trinity team weren't chasing them down. They had swept wide, past the mud banks, moving swiftly to reach the Howard-Aidens fight from the spectator side. If she hadn't stopped to take a breath, they would have all been too busy fighting the St Aiden's siege to notice.

The dwarf had to die, and he had to die right now.

She rushed into the circle around him, and as he sprang forward at somebody's kneecaps (everybody was starting to look the same in red), she pounced herself, wrapping her gauntlet arm around his throat and lifting him up with a grunt. He kicked wildly in the air, and he managed to give a chin a blow that clicked her head back.

A small boy came in and grabbed the siege's arm, trying to hold it fast as it shook with all the strength of the cornered wildcat. *Joseph?* Sarah recognised the meek eyes. The boy had been hanging back for most of the fight, trying not to put himself in the kill-or-be-killed situations the game demanded. But now he was hanging on for dear life.

'Go for it, for fuck's sake!' Sarah yelled, as her hostage bit into her arm, breaking skin. She punched him in the side and met hard muscle.

The other players had been hesitant, kept at bay by the kicking legs, but then Alex and an older boy—was that Christopher?—broke through from the sides, and their two gauntlets together went for the stomach, now held up to an easy reach. The body trembled, and then Sarah's arm, tense and pained, was suddenly without pressure, hanging crooked in the air as though she had been one-arm hugging an invisible friend.

A slab of stringy gore hit her eyes and she bowed her head, blinking furiously as her vision filled with tears.

'Mike, Mike!' she called out.

'I'm here,' he said.

'I can't see a thing. Guard me will you?'

'Already on it.'

'Trinity are coming!' She stabbed her finger in an approximate spot.

'They're already here,' Mike said.

Sarah stood up, backing away from the scarlet blur of figures that clashed in front of her. There was no use wiping her eyes; everything was already covered, if not dripping, in blood. She had to rely on the body's own defence. She kept on blinking, hating the stinging but welcoming the tears.

Bit by bit, she could see.

She saw, between blinks, Mike get bowled over by a Trinity player that had charged him head-down. *Be the matador*, she thought hopelessly. In scrums like this, nobody even knew the meaning of the word finesse.

A gauntlet came through the veil of tears, driving towards her stomach, and her own gauntlet shot out and blocked it. She felt the jolt and shudder as the two vibrations locked, snarling at each other, and then she twisted away, grabbing the opponent's battle arm with her other hand and driving her gauntlet into a young girl's belly.

She closed her eyes this time, turning her head, and felt the meaty splatter on her bare skin, and a rain of small wet thuds on her kit. Her eyes snapped open again, prepared immediately for another attack.

It was all over. There was no field of corpses to survey, no dead players littering the ground. Merely a soggy mush, a red mud that sank between the blades of grass and squished under their boots.

The William Howard team had only six players left. Herself, Mike, Jack, an older girl called Sophie, Joseph, and another boy she couldn't remember the name of, who would soon be gone too, as the nameless often are. Christopher and Alex would not be sharing the celebrations if their team proved victorious, except perhaps in spirit.

The boy Joseph had a thousand-yard stare to him. She was amazed he had lasted this long, but wondered if he was not merely staying out of the fight for the most part. She had not seen him kill anyone. In a way, ever since the showers, she had felt partly responsible for him. This was an unwelcome feeling in this game. You were responsible for all players equally, but (this was the unwritten rule) chiefly your own survival. You did not make new friends, and you did not make better friends out of your existing ones (*Mike, we'll be like this 'till one of us dies*).

Sarah would not watch out for Joseph any more than any other player. If he was dead weight, her attentions were far better spent on herself.

The other William Howard players were tired, winded, and in between catching their breath and surveying the now empty field around them, were talking about what next. Sarah blinked her eyes a few more times, and joined the conversation. Some distance away, some of the crowd were cheering.

Stonewaters Bookstore had spent the entire time in the forests, if they had showed up to the game at all. It was quite likely, Sarah ventured, that the St Aidens and Trinity teams were wiped out, assuming Stonewaters could fight worth a damn. Sophie noted that they still hadn't seen the Trinity siege, the giant. Perhaps he was in the forests, perhaps he was dead.

'And the Stonewaters siege? If they have one?' asked Jack, spitting on the ground.

Sarah shrugged, and turned away, not missing the dirty look Jack gave her. *Keep your mind on the here and now, not on my bare ass,* she thought.

'Do we wait for them to come out, or do we go in the woods?' asked Joseph quietly.

She didn't look at him. 'They're not going to come out,' she said. 'We're going in.'

•   •   •

They heard the giant before they saw him. His stomp was loud, breaking branches and flattening bracken. There was a peculiar rumbling in the ground, with each step as he lurched through the shadowy woods.

She stole a quick glance from behind a tree. The player was huge; not merely tall, but towering, with long, stalk like legs, and elongated forearms that hung far past its waist. His gaunt face was the only part of him not covered in blood; only his chin, which made him look like a diner at a cannibal's feast.

He was also alone.

She sat down fast, and a voice inside her said *there was something else, too, something not right, something you missed,* but her head was too much in the game to dwell on anything more than the single hulking Trinity player heading their way, and an immediate need for tactics. She wasn't going to risk a second look.

'Mike, double up, I'll be top,' Sarah whispered quickly, then turned to the others crouched silently in the undergrowth. 'The rest of you, distract, go for its legs. It can't get you without stooping. It's got defence over offense, remember.'

She sat on Mike's shoulders, and he slowly stood up, his knees knocking slightly. She rose up through the air, a newly-formed giant herself, still half-hidden behind the tree.

She beckoned at Sophie, Jack, Joseph and whoever-he-was, and the four of them rushed out and encircled the giant, Sophie at the lead, Joseph hanging back.

The Trinity player stopped dead, nostrils flaring, then laughed as the Sarah-Mike entity emerged and walked unsteadily in front of him. He rubbed his huge palms together, and flexed the fingers. Something cracked.

'The gauntlet! It's -' started Mike.

'On his foot,' finished Sarah grimly. *That's what I missed. The rumbling on the ground.*

'Is that allowed?' asked Sophie.

'Doesn't really matter right now. Let's blow this son of a bitch.'

Jack rushed in and punched it in back of the thigh, and got a backwards kick in the belly for his trouble. He backed off, retching slightly. The offending foot wasn't gauntleted, or feeling sick would be one of many problems he wouldn't have anymore.

The giant swung with his arms and kicked out with his legs, and all but Sarah-Mike were ducking and diving about, unprepared with such a fighting style. It wasn't martial art, it was too undisciplined and wild for that. But with a killing device on the foot, it was deadly and unpredictable. Sarah-Mike remained at the fringes, skulking between the trees, unwilling to come in and have Mike's leg's kicked away, or Sarah launched off through the air by a sailing fist. She looked desperately for an opening, one good enough for Mike to stagger in quick before the giant turned on them.

The opening they got came at a sacrifice. They saw Sophie grabbed by the arm and dangled in the air. They saw Jack, the nameless boy and even Joseph rush in and hammer at the giant, trying to jump up to get at the stomach, gravity winning every time. They saw the gauntleted foot rise up, and they saw Sophie's face, white through the blood, eyes popping, seeing her own death in that great throbbing foot.

Sarah-Mike were behind the Trinity siege, and she pointed forward, not wanting to yell out the 'NOW!' that was so eager to burst through her lips. She needn't have even pointed, for Mike had already seen the opportunity, and was moving at surprising speed considering his burden.

Sarah wrapped herself around the giant's neck at the same time as Mike drove his gauntlet with all his strength into his back.

The giant yelled out, bending backwards at the same time as Sophie exploded.

Mike twisted to the side, and Sarah, hanging by herself now, pulled the giant down, the two of them hitting the earth together. Sarah's back smacked against the earth, and she felt the pain instantly, but held on tight, choking the giant with the tightness of her arms.

Mike, Jack and the nameless boy all went for the kill, but it was small, timid Joseph who got to the stomach first. A geyser of gore torrented upwards and outwards, covering everything.

There was silence, and for a second you could feel the heartbeat of the forest. Joseph looked at her, nonplussed, his face dripping. Sarah sat up, her back and legs groaning and aching. *That'll hurt in the morning.*

She looked back at Joseph and managed a grin. 'Well done,' she said. She squinted at the trees. 'I hope the cameras got all that.'

Joseph mouth moved upwards into a smile, one that his mind was clearly not participating in. The grin grew broader until it reached its apex, and fixed itself to him with maniacal permanency. It was still stuck to his face when he shuddered, the arm hugging him from behind, the gauntlet pressed against his belly—and he was gone, leaving behind only a patter of flesh and the thought of a smile.

Behind him, a player slowly stood up from the darkness of the undergrowth. She was the braided girl who had spoken from the stage yesterday, and she had the grim, implacable look of the not entirely human.

All around them Stonewaters players in bloodied, camouflage green were standing up, casting aside the leaves and branches that hid them, climbing up from hollows in the ground, leaping down like cats from their perches high in the trees.

Trinity and St Aidens are gone, Sarah knew, shivering under the cold, quietly murderous eyes of their soon-to-be assassins. *And it* looks like Stonewaters have taken hardly any casualties. We're facing nearly an entire team.

Suddenly, she was terrified.

She watched the nameless boy, as scared as her, maybe more so, dealing with his fear by screaming and running at them. She watched as he disappeared, calmly dispatched by a player whose face betrayed no emotion, none but a rigid kind of frenzy that hid behind their eyes.

The boy's name was Peter, she remembered. *He had brown hair, and brown eyes, and his most remarkable moment was bursting apart. Then we really knew what was inside him. The same as everyone.*

She knew what would have been the last thought in Peter's mind, that tiniest hesitation that cost him his life. It would have been the Stonewaters captains, in their mascot outfits: the milk, the bread, the sugar. A shopping list to die for.

Jack and Mike backed away as Stonewaters advanced. Sarah looked about her, her gauntlet hanging loosely at her side, and she did something she'd never done before in a game.

She ran.

She ran from the battle.

She ran from her team mates.

She ran from Mike.

'Sarah!' she heard the cry behind her, but she didn't look around; she was too busy jumping fallen branches, ducking and dodging, and putting her screaming legs to the limit as she sprinted through the darkness.

Gotta stay alive, she repeated to herself, and even the disembodied voice in her head was panting the words. *Can't win if I'm dead*, it shifted to, and she began to convince herself that this was strategy, and not a cowardly, selfish flight.

The trees clustered in closer, and she slowed, eventually coming to a halt when she could no longer hear any signs of pursuit. She walked among the bones of black trees, feeling sick and empty. She snapped off some broad leaves from a plant and tried to wipe some of the muck off her face.

She had lost all sense of direction. She didn't know if she was heading back to the field, or deeper into the woods.

It was starting to get cold. While it might be daylight outside, in here it might as well be night. She inspected the trees closely, but she couldn't see a single camera, and she had a chilling feeling that nobody knew where she was, that she was entirely alone.

The noise was like the creak of a door, or a slowly falling tree, except it wasn't natural, but came from a mouth. It rose in volume, a harpy screech that seemed to come from every nook and pore of the forest.

'Who's there?' Sarah called out, not caring anymore about revealing her position to another player. She wanted to surrender. She wanted to put her arms up, take her gauntlet off and give herself up.

But she knew that you couldn't surrender. Not in this game. If you put your arms up, you were dead.

Then someone, something came out from behind a tree, a tree so thin it seemed impossible it could have hidden her, it. The woman was completely naked, pale as death and almost skeletal. Her bones gleamed slightly, with an almost sickly wet pallor. There was nearly no light, but the woman's popping, owl-ish eyes shone black and white, like polished snooker balls.

The creature was the Stonewaters captain, and she was smiling, impossibly wide and stretched, her rubbery lips coming almost up to her eyeballs. The teeth had come out from the gums, and were now as long as fingers, as thin as twigs and as sharp as stakes.

Sarah couldn't breathe. Her feet were stuck to the ground. She saw the pale monster reach out her spindly arms, holding them outstretched before her. The fingers, like the teeth, were longer than before, and were growing before her eyes. The fingers came out like a network of roots blossoming in fast forward through the earth. They crept through the air towards her, multiplying in crooked joints with every few inches gained. As they grew, they creaked and rasped.

Sarah screamed then, trailing off in a whimper when she saw the huge eyes light up, as though inner delight fed the torch that burned behind those black-white bulbs.

The creature licked its lips with a slimy black tongue.

'We took care of the cameras, dearie,' said the creature in a voice like a saw. 'Nobody sees when we don't want them to.'

The two other captains appeared from behind poles of bark to either side of the woman, both as naked, like sharp white stick figures animated out from black line trees.

140

They were smiling too.

Sarah heard the drone, the sound that had replayed in her head since yesterday, since listening to the captains stood tall and grinning on that stage. That flat buzzing sound that now came from everywhere, came from inside her, trembling like worms in her veins and flies in her guts.

She put her hands over her ears, but the droning, the creaking, the screech of the captains was not muffled. The woman's fingers had reached her now, tickling her chest and neck. The fingertips curled and tried to hook her, to snag her flesh.

The droning was increasing in volume, and Sarah imagined a brush in her mind, a hard thin broom with fingers for bristles, sweeping away the clutter of her thoughts, sweeping away her horror, slowly leaving her mind's corridors and halls polished and empty, with only the scrape of fingernails to mark them.

The terror faded, and numbness washed through her. The woman's groaning fingers tickled her mouth, trying to pry her lips open so they could come inside.

The finger-broom in her mind opened the doors to her memories, and advanced.

No, said the voice in her mind. It was a strong voice, a tough, angry voice. *These are mine,* it said. *Hands off what's mine.*

The finger-broom tried to usher it away, but the shadow behind the voice stood firm and blocked the corridor.

Sarah's eyes were shut fast, and in response to the voice her mouth tightened against the finger.

I'm a survivor, said the voice. *Where everybody dies, I live.* The shadow behind the voice kicked the broom, and it scuttled back.

Sarah opened her eyes. With a numb hand she grabbed the finger, and snapped the end.

The woman howled, and the hand pulled back, the joints popping back into themselves as the fingers withdrew.

Sarah was moving. Her whole body felt like it'd been packed in snow. Her legs obeyed the shadow's command because they knew otherwise they would not exist. Her arms obeyed the shadow's command because they knew otherwise they would not exist.

Her brain, her dull, grey lobes working on instinct alone obeyed the shadow's command, because it wasn't given a choice.

Her dead body moved faster than she knew how, and her gauntlet was up, and then it was in the woman's stomach.

Sarah stared into those bulbous eyes, at that giant fanged grin that just now began to quiver and shake.

There was a cascade of black blood and bits that swam around her feet.

Suddenly Sarah was alone. The two male captains had disappeared. The woman had dripped her way into Sarah's socks.

Everything rushed back into her. Her limbs shook and she fell to the ground. Her mind took control, was filled up again, and the shadow and its voice retreated, nodding its way out.

•   •   •

Sarah walked back through the forest. She didn't know how far she was walking, in what direction, or how long it was taking. She was making the most of having her mind back, whilst trying to control her shakes.

Milk, bread and sugar. Fingers like the branches of a tree. Smiles. Black bits around my feet.

'Sarah!'

Sarah raised her head. Mike was there, standing in a circle of gore. He was grinning widely, seemingly forgotten her betrayal.

'What the hell happened?' she said, amazed to see him alive.

'They killed Jack. They were coming for me. Then, they just stopped. They just . . . gave up. I've no idea!'

She looked around. 'So you killed them all.'

'It was like shooting fish in a barrel. I just went up to them and blew them one by one. They didn't even fight back.'

'It was the captains. I found them in the woods. They . . . they were fucked up. They weren't human.'

Mike gaped at her. 'What happened?'

'They tried to take me over. I . . . I don't understand what happened. They got into my mind. But I resisted them. And I killed one of them, the woman. I think she led the others. They disappeared at the same time. I don't know where they went, if they are gone forever or just escaped.'

'Wow,' said Mike. 'Then . . . I guess you take the head, the rest of the snake goes with it.'

'They were brainwashed,' said Sarah. 'They were controlled. Had their minds taken over. When the captains deserted them, their minds were left empty. Maybe they'd have got them back in time, maybe not. But they're gone now.'

'Do you realise what this means? It means we've won!'

Sarah shook her head, feeling so utterly exhausted. She just wanted to lie down. 'We haven't. They haven't sounded the end of the game. The siren.'

Mike's face fell. 'Then . . .'

Sarah's gaze shifted to left and behind of Mike. 'And there she is,' she said flatly. 'The Stonewaters siege.'

Mike span around, and the both of them looked through the trees to see a girl watching them. She looked about seventeen, and she was very, very pregnant.

'Oh fuck,' said Mike.

Sarah sat down, as the last Stonewaters player walked slowly towards them.

'What are you doing?' said Mike.

'I can't do this.'

Mike sat down next to her. 'It's okay.'

'I know.'

'I don't think there's anything in the rules, you know. About using a pregnant player. I don't know. Nobody's ever done it before.' He paused to think. 'Clever, though.'

'Clever?'

'Yeah. Nobody would want to target her.'

The girl was almost upon them, her arms hanging loosely at her sides. She was staring dully ahead, her face vacant.

'She might not be pregnant,' added Mike, unconvincingly. 'It might be a trick. Something covering her belly. It'd be against the rules, though. Though it sounds like the Stonewaters have been playing fucked from the start.'

Sarah didn't say anything.

'I bet she's not pregnant. It's fake.'

Sarah stood up, and Mike followed.

The girl stopped in front of them, her protruding belly just a few inches from Sarah. They stared into each other's eyes, but the girl wasn't really seeing.

'Do it,' said Mike quietly, urgently. 'Do it.'

Sarah waved a hand in front of the girl, and the eyes flickered.

A Stonewaters gauntlet drew back, and instinctually, Sarah's own gauntlet caught the player in the stomach.

THRUM

•   •   •

Sarah and Mike walked out of the woods, back onto the field. The siren had sounded, and spectators were cheering loudly, and waving banners with the William Howard School crest. Others had their heads in their hands.

'We're heroes, Sarah,' said Mike. He tried to reach for her hand, to pull it to the sky, but she moved away.

'I'm done,' she said, knowing she was still shaking. 'I don't understand what happened today, and I don't want to understand. No more.' She took a deep breath. 'Too much blood. It's been too much blood. For today. For every day.'

Mike gave a short, bewildered laugh. 'There's never too much blood Sarah.'

She didn't say anything more, and they walked on in silence towards their victory celebrations.

JANUARY 5TH

I t was January the 5th, and everywhere things were dead or dying.

The skim of the water shivered its way downstream; on a night so chill and mystical even the river had goosebumps. He put his hand on the walls of the bridge and felt the weight: as above, so below.

The path led him, pulled him by the hand, along and along. He trailed the bushes, pricked thorns. Red-black buds bloomed on his fingertips and he let them drip.

January 5th, a new year.

The river followed him like a hungry dog. On the far bank was a long line of mops: huge and shaggy heads of hair swaying side to side, their eyes and faces lost in darkness. A run of giants and every one shaking their heads at him.

'It's just . . . I don't know how to be happier,' the pauper boy said in the corner of his eye. 'Or, just, happy more often.'

'Well, that's because life isn't a search for joy and happiness son,' replied the weathered old gentleman standing by the boy.

The two figures shifted in stop-motion to keep up with the corner of his eye. He didn't look right at them, for he knew if he did they would disappear.

'It isn't?' the pauper boy said, looking up with big innocent eyes that flashed with something's reflection.

The gentleman patted the boy on the shoulder. 'No,' he said. 'It's a challenge. The ultimate challenge. The last levels.'

'There are more than one?'

'Perhaps. Each more difficult than the last. Life by life it will become harder, crueller, and life by life you will appreciate it more. Eventually you will get to the final level, and you will have encountered the very depths of wickedness, cruelty and injustice, and you will never have more love and respect for life.'

'And then what?'

'And then you win.'

'Is that it? For all that? Is there no reward?'

The old man stared out into the night, as if he knew they were being watched. 'Perhaps there is,' he said.

SUBSCRIBE TO EVERYTHING WE PUBLISH!

Do you love what Microcosm publishes?

Do you want us to publish more great stuff?

Would you like to receive each new title as it's published?

Subscribe as a BFF to our new titles and we'll mail them all to you as they are released!

$10-30/mo, pay what you can afford. Include your t-shirt size and your birthday for a possible surprise!

microcosmpublishing.com/bff

...AND HELP US GROW YOUR SMALL WORLD!

Other Books by Set Sytes: